Bruyere Publishing
c/o Michael Schmidt
11526 Sorrento Valley Road, Suite A-2
San Diego, CA 92121

For information regarding special discounts for bulk purchases and author appearances, call 858-509-0582 x 250 or email MMJS@TALENTSMART.COM

ISBN: 978-0974320663
First Printing: 2013

Printed and assembled in the United States of America.

This book is dedicated to Maribel, my biggest fan.

1.

I didn't have the slightest inkling I was going to die that day. Though some will argue that I didn't really experience death. The blood stopped coursing through my veins—this much is certain—just as it will some day for you, but there were no pearly gates, no departed loved ones guiding me into the light. While I was away, I experienced nothingness. Perhaps this was intentional, as the great cosmic scorekeeper knew I wasn't finished walking the earth.

I awoke to the dry howl of Santa Ana winds that snaked down through the coastal canyons on their way out to sea. The sagging backs of aging patio chairs fluttered nervously on the porch. I lived in a shingled Craftsman, with a sprawling deck that sat perilously on the edge of a tall sandstone bluff overlooking the Pacific Ocean. A few years before, I'd outbid uppity suburbanites and wealthy retirees for the home. They'd have to find their status symbol elsewhere. I had but one favorite wave in San Diego, and my home was perched directly above it.

I yanked the handle on the sliding door and stepped outside. The cold wind sent the hair on my bare arms bristling to attention. I took a gulp from my steaming morning coffee and observed the expectant crowd bobbing up and down amidst the crashing surf below. Most mornings, I would nurse my coffee and lament the burgeoning surfing population. I'd long for the days when a man could hit the waves with nothing but the dolphins to keep him company. But there was no bellyaching today; I had better plans.

My phone buzzed in my pocket. I pulled it out and fumbled about before flicking it open with my thumb.

"You up?" my son Colt's voice buzzed from the tiny speaker.

"I'm here in the car. Just about to start 'er up," I lied.

"All right, see you there."

I snapped the phone shut between my cheek and shoulder and took a final gulp from my coffee. I slammed the mug down onto the porch railing and scurried down the patio steps toward the open garage. Surfboards and wetsuits were strewn about as if the place had been ransacked. I grabbed what I needed and slid the boards and neoprene into the back of my truck.

I threw the truck into gear and raced down the driveway. When I reached the bottom, I stomped on the brake and threw the truck into park. I hopped out of the truck and ran back up to the house through a biting gust of wind. I never left the house without kissing my wife first.

She was curled up in the living room lounge chair reading a book. The rising sun cast a warm glow through the window behind her that made her look angelic. I snuck up behind her and draped my arms around her neck.

"Royce Bruyere, what *are* you doing?" she cooed.

"Just saying bye."

She dropped her book into her lap, turned, and kissed me on the mouth. "Be careful out there today, OK? I don't like the sound of that wind."

"I will. I promise. See you at eight sharp."

When I pulled into the airfield parking lot, Colt was already inspecting the plane. A six-seater, the Cessna 206 was a lot of airplane for a guy who'd just earned his pilot's license, but it left plenty of room for surfboards. Besides, I could afford it. I'd spent two decades building a software company from the ground up. Most of my competitors had lost fistfuls of other people's cash, along with their companies, during the dot-com bubble, but I never succumbed to the temptation. I believed in bootstrapping it and being the master of your own destiny. These days, I spent more time in the water than in the office.

Colt leaned against the plane's protruding cowl while he checked the propeller blades for nicks. He was too focused on the task to see me walking toward him. I couldn't help but admire my son. He looked much like I had in my early twenties—wide in the shoulders but lanky with long swinging arms like a gorilla. Colt's jaw was wide and masculine, his face dotted with thick overgrown stubble. Bleached-blond tips of hair wormed out beneath his ball cap and fluttered in the wind.

"She ready?" I asked.

"Yup. Everything checks out."

I ran my hand delicately along the leading edge of the wing. Colt clasped my shoulder and jerked the door open.

"Come on, old man. Let's get to it!"

Colt wore the halo of an only child. If he said the plane checked out, it was ready. Colt's belongings rested neatly in the rear of the plane. I hustled to follow suit. I slipped my boards inside, threw wetsuits and bags on top, and jumped into the pilot's seat. Most men my age lacked the spunk needed for a spur-of-the-moment surf trip with a twenty year old. I was narrowing in on fifty, but a lifetime consumed with surfing meant I looked and felt a decade younger. I was fit with a head of thick salt and pepper hair and light blue eyes that were a stark contrast to my sun-bronzed skin. My wife always said what attracted her to me was that I was blissfully unaware of my good looks. I thought she was just flattering me.

I put my headset on, cleared my throat, and prepared to fly. When I turned the key, the engine choked slightly before firing up. The propeller roared to life and settled into an even hum. Moments later, we were bouncing down the runway. I eased back on the yoke, and the plane leapt into the air.

We soared high until we crossed the border into Mexico, where we swung low above the rugged coastline of Northern Baja. The sea was a pristine sheet of cobalt blue that stretched out to the horizon. Beneath us, a winter swell finished its three-thousand-mile journey from the heart of a storm near the Aleutians. The waves traveled together in uniform corduroy lines that rose tall as they rolled toward the shoreline.

"Look at that, Dad . . . it's firing," Colt crowed with his nose pressed against the glass.

"You ready for this?" I asked. "We'll be on the ground in an hour."

Colt glared at me, scarcely taking his eyes off the water.

"What? You still been getting waves, what with finals and all?"

"Of course. I've always got time for a surf."

I grew warm with pride. This was a young man who had his priorities straight. We marveled at the scene below us with only the vibrating hum of the engine breaking the silence.

We touched down in bouncing fits on a dusty airstrip in the middle of nowhere, its boundaries peppered with cacti and low-lying shrubs. The sandy dirt runway was soft and rutted. The only structure in sight was a weathered wooden lean-to alongside a rusting gas pump.

As I parked the plane at the end of the runway, a tall Ford pickup with oversized tires came tearing down a small hill in our direction. I stretched over the seat into the back of the plane and grabbed a small duffel. The truck slid to a halt alongside us. A leg sporting a cowboy boot deftly kicked the door open, and the truck's undersized occupant hopped out and landed firmly in the dust below.

"¡Nacho!" I exclaimed. "¿Que onda gordo?"

I was overjoyed by the sight of my old friend. Nacho was an ancient Mexican cowboy. His face bore deep lines and a withered complexion that exposed his age in ways his taut, muscular physique could not. A vigorous handshake quickly morphed into a man hug with lots of back patting.

"Where you been, *güero*? How come you no visit México?"

"Ay, no swell, amigo. No swell."

"I had to drive you truck three times to keep the báteria working."

"I know, I know. I'd rather be here than there, believe me, but the point doesn't work unless it's six foot. Oh, hey! I brought something for ya."

I reached into the duffel and pulled out a bottle of Kentucky bourbon. Nacho held the bottle of bourbon up with both hands and admired it as if it were a child.

"Ay, Don Royce, thank you. Good boorbon no es easy to find here."

"I have something else for you, too, buddy."

I handed Nacho a Three Tenors CD.

"¡Los Tres Tenores! Gracias."

Nacho paused. "¿Pues, no quieren surfiar?"

Nacho had a point. It was nice to catch up, but we were burning precious daylight. I motioned to Colt. "Let's go hit it so we can get back before dark. You know how much Mom hates us flying at night."

We loaded our gear in the truck and drove Nacho back to his ranch. Nacho hopped out and wished us well. I peeled out in the dirt and headed toward the beach.

"Dad?"

"Yeah."

"Why do you call Ignacio, Nacho?" Colt's fingers danced nervously on the dashboard.

"What do you mean?"

"It just doesn't seem right to call him that."

"Would you prefer I call him taco?" I kept my eyes fixed on the dirt road that wound back and forth through the chaparral. "Or maybe burrito?"

Colt swallowed. "It's just that I took this course on cultural diversity, and it sounds condescending. It'd be like him calling you hamburger or something."

"Or mac n' cheese . . . no, no it'd be like him calling me pancakes."

I threw Colt a quick grin that failed to penetrate his contemplation. His pursuit was so earnest that I felt bad for leading him along.

"Hey, knucklehead. Let me ask you something," I said.

"K."

"Did they teach you that Nacho is short for Ignacio in that diversity class of yours?"

Colt looked confused and uncomfortable. I reached over and tussled his hair.

"Aww, come on, pal. I was just having some fun with you. I know you're only trying to keep me honest, and I appreciate that. I really do."

Colt grinned sheepishly.

"Now, let's go get some surf, ya?" I asked, pushing harder on the gas.

After six miles of winding through the chaparral kicking up dust and chattering over washboard roads, we emerged at a sandy point sticking a half-mile out into the ocean. The waves peeled perfectly along the promontory, one after another in orderly sets of eight. Not a drop of water was out of place.

Colt and I were quick to succumb to the itchy paranoia that plagues surfers hoping to protect quality waves. We climbed the running boards on opposite sides of the truck and craned our necks north and south looking for any sign of other surfers. The point was usually occupied by groups of campers, but today it was empty. Not a board floating in the water and not a soul standing on the beach. We could scarcely contain ourselves.

Minutes of bliss melted into hours of ecstasy as my son and I traded waves. We stood on our surfboards in succession, each racing a wave down the point, drifting up and down on backlit teal walls of water. Each wave was flawless, depositing its rider nearly a minute after it started a good half-mile down the point. The fastest way to another ride was to run on the beach back up the point. A long afternoon of successive journeys on this conveyor belt of bliss left our legs shaking and our arms hanging dead at our sides. We dragged our hanging flesh up to the truck and struggled out of our wetsuits.

The sun was hanging low on the horizon as we left the beach and made our way toward Nacho's ranch. We found Nacho breaking bales of alfalfa in the back of a beat-up '72 Chevrolet pickup. He chuckled at the sight of our bloodshot eyes and the two-toned wetsuit tan on our necks.

"You have fun out in the sewage?"

"Best day ever."

"By far."

Nacho pulled himself up into the truck, and Colt slid over to make room for him. The truck bounced and chattered toward the airstrip.

"You see any brown soobmarines in the water today?"

We were too exhausted to respond to Nacho's joke. I could see him eying our sunken eyes and limp sagging frames with great concern.

"Is getting muy late, eh? Stay tonight at the ranchita. Blanca is making your favorite . . . carnitas."

The mere mention of Blanca's cooking conjured images of braised, pulled pork so vivid I could smell the savory meat, even feel it melting in my mouth.

"That sounds really—"

"No can do," I said, interrupting Colt. "Date night tonight."

"Aw, Dad. There's no way we're gonna make it home on time."

"She'll forgive me for being late, but she'll kill me for blowing her off."

Colt loaded the airplane while I topped it off with fuel. The sun dipped into the ocean, and the sudden change in temperature sprung howling winds to life. I released the lever on the pump handle and returned it to the cradle. I shoved the numb hand into my pocket, which provided little protection from the biting gusts.

I climbed into the cockpit and started working the instrument panel in preparation for takeoff. Nacho approached the plane and opened my door.

"You sure you don't want to stay here, amigo?" Nacho urged. "Es muy windy to be flying this plane."

"No, no . . . we'll be fine. I've done this before." I started the engine. "We should be getting some more swell soon," I yelled over the engine noise. "How 'bout a rain check on those carnitas?"

"Ok, Don Royce. You be careful, eh?"

I smiled and winked and pulled the door shut.

"You got this?" Colt asked, looking at me nervously.

"Yeah, no worries. We'll be home before you know it."

We had a smooth takeoff despite the push and pull of the devil wind. Our flight through Mexico was uneventful, much as it had been in the opposing direction that morning. However, not long after we crossed the border, the wind took a turn for the worse. By the time I could see the runway lights in the distance, the onslaught of wind was punctuated by violent gusts that stopped as suddenly as they started. I looked over at Colt, who was listening to music on his oversized headphones. The expression on his face was sublime. Colt believed me when I said there was nothing to worry about.

A gust of wind sent the plane shimmying to the left. The abrupt movement snapped my attention back to the approaching runway. The wind was blowing in from the east, but the runway ran northbound. I thought back to what I'd practiced in flight school, and pointed the nose of the plane into the wind. Every time I lined the runway up in the center of the windshield, a gust of wind would send the plane veering off to the left. My throat grew tight with the impending touchdown. I felt a squeezing sensation deep in my chest. The cockpit seemed smaller and hotter the closer we came to the runway. As I braced the yoke for landing, a massive burst of wind took hold of the plane. I pushed the Cessna hard into the gust to keep us over the center of the runway, but the wind released the plane a moment before the wheels touched ground, and I had no time to compensate. The plane's windward momentum sent us careening off the runway. I tried furiously to complete the landing even though we went bouncing off into the darkness, but the wheels wouldn't stay on the ground and the plane refused to level. The tip of the wing on Colt's side caught asphalt first, vaulting the entire plane into a lumbering cartwheel. When the nose met the ground, it crushed the propeller into the crumpled cowl. The impact absorbed the bulk of the plane's momentum, and when the tail came around it gripped the pavement enough to flop the plane back onto its belly where it skidded to a halt.

I couldn't see Colt through the dust and smoke. I struggled to free myself from my seatbelt but was overcome by a crushing pain in my chest. It felt as if my upper body were locked in a vice. My mind slowed and my vision blurred. All I could do was think of Colt. Colt was young and vibrant; he had his whole life ahead of him. I felt reckless and ashamed. All I'd ever wanted to do was provide for my son, and I'd thrown it all away. I'd succumbed to my own impulsivity and insisted on flying home. Now that decision had robbed Colt of everything.

"Dad, Dad, are you all right?"

Someone grabbed me and dragged me from the plane onto the ground.

"Talk to me, Dad, please!"

The blurry apparition above me pulled back far enough that I could make out Colt's face. Tears streamed down Colt's bloodstained cheeks as he struggled to perform chest compressions on me. A thin smile washed across my lips as I slipped away.

2.

The blood surged through my body, filling the narrow reaches of craggy capillaries that had long lain dormant. I awoke to an intense burning and itching as nerve endings sprang to life violently beneath my leather dry skin. A group of wooden Asian men in pressed ivory lab coats stood around the bed. They shared observations with one another in short powerful bursts of Chinese. I was in too much pain to react to their repressed enthusiasm.

"Can you hear me? Do you hear me, Mister Brooyear?" one of the men asked, flicking a flashlight on and off into each of my eyes.

I struggled to move. My body twitched like a seizure, sending a burning sensation deep into my muscles. This spasm further excited the men who leaned over me and watched my eyes dance about. The pain grew excruciating. I felt as if I was burning alive. A hoarse guttural yell erupted from deep inside. The men leapt back nervously. The man with the flashlight barked an order. Another man pulled a syringe from his pocket and injected the contents into one of the many tubes protruding from my body. Four agonizing seconds later, I lost consciousness.

3.

I awoke comfortably a few days later in a stark room that was blindingly white from floor to ceiling. Roughly the size of a three-car garage, the room was far too large for its contents—several pieces of unfamiliar medical equipment and the bed I lay in. A sizeable pane of observation glass separated the room from the outside hallway. I sat up and rubbed my eyes. My skin felt moist and supple. I was surprised I could move my arms back and forth with scarcely a hint of soreness. I was dressed in a shiny, metallic gown that was loose and soft.

The door opened with a loud beep, and a short Caucasian guy in blue scrubs walked in. He looked to be in his early thirties. His large brown cow eyes matched his frumpy chestnut hair, and his puffy cheeks overpowered his small, flat chin.

"How does it feel to be alive?" the man asked.

"Never known anything different."

"Sense of humor intact." The man smiled at me and leaned awkwardly against the bed.

"What's so funny about that?"

"You know, *you have never known anything different . . .*"

"What are you trying to say? Did I have to be resuscitated after the plane crash or something?"

"Oh, OK, now I understand." The man's cheerful expression turned serious, but I wasn't sure why. He sat down at the foot of the bed.

"Your name is Royce, right?"

"Yeah."

"I'm Alex."

"Nice to meet you, Alex. Now are you going to tell me what in the hell happened to me?"

"I can tell you what I know about your case. If you need more information than that, I suppose you can try speaking with the doctors."

"So you're not a doctor?"

"No. I'm a technician."

"What kind of technician?"

"Cryogenics."

I didn't like hearing that word. I lost focus and found myself staring right through Alex.

"Do you realize you signed up for cryopreservation?"

I nodded slightly.

"You died after a plane crash. You suffered a heart attack."

"But I'm not dead."

"Not anymore. We brought you back to life."

"Are you serious?"

"Absolutely. You were frozen for . . ." Alex stared at the ceiling while he performed the math in his head, "a good thirty-five years."

"Holy . . ." My thoughts evaporated, and the room started spinning. Then it hit me. I looked at Alex and burst into hysterical laughter.

"You son of a bitch!" I gave Alex a playful shove on the shoulder. "You're fucking with me, aren't you? Who put you up to this? Was it Gary? That guy never misses an opportunity to bust my balls over wanting to get frozen."

I looked around the room. "That bastard really went all out." I pinched the front of my gown and lifted the fabric toward Alex. "I mean, look at this thing!"

The men in the white coats now stood outside in the hallway. As soon as Alex saw them, his expression turned dire and his voice stern. "This is not a practical joke."

"Come on, man. I've been through a lot. Just let me see my wife and son."

"Listen to me. When they come in here, do not tell them what I told you. I'm not even supposed to be talking to you. Just do everything they say, and you'll be fine."

I rolled my eyes.

"Just do what they say, all right? I'll come back later. I promise."

Alex jumped up and started to fiddle with the machine next to my bed. He shuffled out with his head down as soon as the men in the white coats entered the room. At first, they stood near the doorway and marveled like I was some kind of exotic animal. One man pointed at me and shared an observation that sent the group into a flurry of debate. They repeated this dumbfounding cycle multiple times before approaching me.

"Feeling better, Mister Brooyear?" the man with the flashlight asked. The others deferred to him.

"Better than when?"

"The last time we saw you, of course."

"Yes, you could say that. Seeing as how I'm no longer on fire."

My irritation vexed the man in charge. "Yes, an unfortunate complication of reanimation. A small price to pay for being alive, wouldn't you agree?"

"Not so sure about that. I mean, I didn't go to medical school or anything, but I never heard of anyone burning alive just because they had a heart attack."

"Mister Brooyear—"

"Royce. You can call me Royce."

The man in charge gave me a caustic smile. "Yes . . . Royce." His tone was acerbic. "Your demeanor is precisely what I would expect in an American from your era. Indeed, you did not study medicine. You were a capitalist, were you not?"

"Still am. Aren't we all?" My comment spawned sideways glances and laughter from the men in the ivory coats.

"Well then, it appears that you will have to rely on the care we provide. And you *are* in *remarkable* condition for a man who has been cryopreserved for nearly forty years." He looked at his minions. They nodded in approval. "Your vital signs are perfect, and we were able to return your skin's elasticity. How does it feel, your skin?"

"Ya, about this whole charade you've got going on here. Don't you think it's a little much?"

"I know nothing about this charade you speak of," the man in charge bellowed.

He and his cohort seemed confused and even offended by my comment. This confused me.

"Look, dude, I'm not buying it. I know I haven't been frozen and brought back to life."

"This is not a game, Mister Brooyear. You are a zenith of scientific discovery. You are the first cryonic *ever* to be successfully reanimated. Schoolchildren millennia from now will learn your name."

The dramatic bullshit he was feeding me only strengthened my resolve that this nightmare was all just an elaborate prank. "So you say I was dead for four decades, and you brought me back to life. What year does that make this?"

"Two thousand forty-seven."

"Ok, Doc. If it's twenty forty-seven, then where are all the cool gizmos? Show me a flying car."

"A what?" One of the other men whispered in the man in charge's ear. "Uh, now I understand, Mister Brooyear."

"Royce."

"You want me to prove to you that this is the future, Royce?"

I nodded.

The man in charge reached into the pocket of his lab coat and pulled out a small metallic cylinder, the size of an AA battery. He pointed the cylinder at me, and it emitted a three-dimensional hologram of an anatomical male.

"You see this, Mister Brooyear? This is an image of you. I can see every aspect of your anatomy. You see this? This is your skin. Now, this, this is your skeletal structure. You broke your right femur as an adolescent, did you not?"

I nodded. He adjusted the position of his index finger on the cylinder, and the hologram displayed my internal organs.

"Here is your heart, and these are your coronary arteries." The image zoomed in on an artery and passed right through the arterial wall. The perspective was amazing, and the image crystal clear. It was as if we were cruising along inside my artery. "See how they are free of plaque? When we corrected your condition, we gave you a fresh start." He adjusted the perspective. "Now look here, you know what this is?"

"Looks like a lung."

"Correct. You see this dense mass here? You have a small hamartoma."

"Terrific. So why didn't you use your super science to take that thing out?"

"You are a smart one. The tumor is benign. It will not be causing you any difficulties." He shut the hologram down with a look of pure satisfaction and returned it to his pocket. He stared at me and folded his arms. "You did not have anything like that in twenty ten, now did you?"

"Actually, doc, I'm not impressed. I saw one of those things in *Star Wars*."

He reeled back. A minion gasped audibly, and others shook their heads. The man who had explained the flying car reference leaned in deferentially toward the man in charge to explain *Star Wars*. He was furious. He reminded me of a cartoon character who was about to boil over and shoot steam from his ears. Pushing his buttons was a real treat. I leaned back comfortably against my pillow.

"You want to see something special, do you?"

He barked orders at the history buff who scurried out of the room. The man in charge stood there stoically. It made me uneasy to see how quickly he'd grown calm.

The history buff burst back into the room holding a scalpel and a handheld device that looked like a credit card reader. He handed them to the man in charge who nodded at the others. They held me down. He stepped on a lever on the floor. Wide plastic straps lashed out from beneath the bed and wrapped around my shoulders, waist, and knees to pin me to the mattress. He stretched a rubber surgical glove over each hand slowly and deliberately.

"I am going to show you something that you will never forget." He took the scalpel from the history buff and placed it gingerly on the thickest part of my right forearm.

"What are you doing?" I screamed.

"Welcome to the future," he said with a caustic smile.

I watched in horror as he pushed on the scalpel until it punctured the skin. A stream of blood ran down my elbow onto the bleached bed sheet. I felt a surge of adrenaline and struggled violently to free myself from the straps. It was useless.

"Please, no, no. Stop!" I pleaded.

He didn't even look up. He dragged the scalpel down the length of my forearm, stopping just above the wrist. The arm pulled apart on either side of the blade, exposing white pustules of fat above thick sinewy braids of muscle tissue. Blood spilled from both sides of the incision and pooled on the mattress before dripping to the floor.

He returned the scalpel to the history buff, who passed him the mysterious handheld device. With nervous apprehension, my bulging eyeballs followed every move he made. They felt as if they might leap out of their sockets to try and stop him. He placed the device at the top of the wound. The device whirred and buzzed, and I felt a tingling against my skin. He tapped buttons. It let out a loud beep, and he pushed the device slowly along the wound site, just as he had moments before with the scalpel. I thought I was hallucinating. The wound trailing the machine closed and completely healed. When it reached my wrist, he turned the machine off and pulled it away. The only evidence of the trauma was a light, slightly elevated scar, much like what you'd expect to see after years of healing. The physical pain that remained was insignificant, but the emotional scars were deep. I released the tension from my muscles and lay there in silence, paying no heed to my captors.

He stood above my head. He methodically removed his gloves, tugging at each finger in a cadence that punctuated his comment. "Tell me, Mister Brooyear, did you enjoy your flying car?"

When I failed to respond, he knelt and whispered into my ear, "I want you to understand something, Mister Brooyear;

I can return you to your prior state just as easily as I brought you out of it. Think of this the next time you are feeling clever."

He stood up, and the men in the white coats left the room.

4.

The men left me strapped to the bed for several hours. The room was absolutely silent as I lay there contemplating my predicament. I was quick to come to terms with the facts that I had thus far refused to allow—I had, indeed, died the night of the plane crash and been brought back to life. When I signed up to be cryogenically frozen, I was too busy living to give it much thought. I figured on the odd chance cryogenics did somehow work, coming back to life would be a lot of fun. It'd be exciting. Bonus time. This was nothing of the sort.

The door's harsh signal broke my concentration. It was Alex, and his raspy voice put me at ease.

"Oh, no. What did they do to you?"

I wasn't sure where to begin. Alex stepped on the pedal, and the straps retreated beneath the bed.

"I wish you had listened to me. You do not want to push their buttons. They want me to get some solid food in you and get you moving around a bit. You up for it?"

I nodded solemnly, sat up, and slid my legs over the edge of the bed. Vertigo kicked in immediately. I clutched the mattress with both hands to keep from falling over. Alex grabbed me by the shoulders and helped me get my feet on the floor. As I stood and Alex helped me take my first tentative steps, my balance was off, but my legs felt strong. As we worked our way out into the hallway, the dizziness subsided, and walking felt downright normal.

"What on earth did they do to me to get me like this? Shouldn't my muscles be weak from all those years as a human popsicle?"

"Fascinating, isn't it?" Alex replied.

"It is, but how'd they do it?"

"Oh, I'm not privy to all the details of their work, but it was likely a combination of activated tissue regeneration and transplants. There are some amazing technologies for healing the body these days."

Alex led me down the hallway. Just like my room, the corridor was bleak. There were no windows, no pictures on the wall, not even signs on the doors. Everyone I saw was Asian, and they all wore the same blank expression and attire as the men in white coats. There was a small sitting room at the end of the hallway with a table and chairs and a large vending machine. Its video screen broken up into nine squares, each containing an image of a plated noodle dish.

"What do you like?" Alex asked.

I pointed at the center image. It was a plate of shredded pork with garlic sprouts on a fluffy bed of noodles. "That pork?"

"Yes."

"I'll take it."

Alex placed his hand on a sensor on the side of the machine. It scanned his fingerprints. The computerized female voice replied, "Welcome, Alex Carter."

Alex touched the image of my dish, and the machine whirred. The whirring was joined by a loud hissing sound. Several seconds later, a pane of tinted glass slid open beneath the display and out slid the steaming hot dish, complete with chopsticks. The pork was plump and moist, the garlic sprouts a bright shade of green, and the noodles thick. It smelled delicious.

"This is organic, right?" I asked playfully. Alex looked confused.

I sighed and sat at the table. "Supposed to be a joke," I muttered under my breath. I grabbed the food with the chopsticks and shoveled a bite into my mouth. The dish was bursting with flavor. "Oh my God, this is good." My eyes rolled up. It was the first pleasure I'd felt since coming back to life.

Alex watched me intently. He looked like he had something to say but was holding back.

"So where's all the other people you guys Frankensteined?" I asked through a mouthful of food.

"You are the first successful reanimation."

"Atta boy, Al. You finally got one of my jokes."

"Everyone knows Frankenstein."

"So they do, Al. So they do." I paused to swallow. "Why me?"

"The circumstances surrounding your death were ideal for reanimation. Your passenger performed CPR until paramedics arrived. They did the same all the way to the hospital. You were DOA, but the passenger notified Restora and the cryonics team was already there waiting. They initiated Active-Compression-Decompression-High-Impulse CPR—"

"Hold on there, Rainman. What did they do to me?"

"The procedures were not explained to you when you signed up for cryopreservation?"

"Sure, sure, they explained it, but that doesn't mean I remember everything. All I know is I had a better shot if I was in one piece and they got to me while I was still fresh."

"That is precisely what happened. The Active-Compression-Decompression-High-Impulse CPR maintained ninety percent arterial oxygen saturation until—"

I put down my chopsticks and folded my arms before exhaling deeply through my nose.

"Fine. You had as much oxygen in your blood as you would if you were flying in an airplane. This ensured that you were biologically viable when cryopreservation was initiated."

"That passenger you mentioned—that's my son. Is he still alive? I need to know where he is." I leaned forward.

"I'm sorry. I don't. After you mentioned him and your wife this morning, I went through all of your files to see if any information about them remained. It was all deleted."

I leapt up from the table. "What do you mean it was deleted? What the fuck is wrong with you people?"

Alex was too alarmed to speak. I started pacing about the tiny room. "I was told they would keep in contact with any surviving family—no matter how much time passed—so that I could be with them."

"I'm sorry. I really am. It's just that—"

"It's bullshit. That's what it is. They promised I would only be brought back to a high quality of life, not to end up as some mad scientist's lab rat. If Restora ever wants another person to sign up for this shit, they better get their act together, quick."

"I'm afraid that's impossible."

"Oh really, Al. Impossible? Who's running Restora these days? Let me speak to him. I'll show you what's possible. They'll run this place like a real hospital where patient records are important and doctors have bedside manner. And windows, for fuck's sake."

"Royce, Restora no longer exists."

"I don't care what the damn company is called these days. Just get me to whoever is in charge."

"Listen, Restora no longer exists because they were . . . *we were* taken over by the Chinese."

"I'm not surprised. They'd already taken over plenty of companies when I was still alive. Are you telling me the Chinese have no interest in customer service?"

"I'm not saying a Chinese interest took over the company. What I'm telling you is China, the country, took over the United States. The part you're in, anyway."

The feeling returned that I had when the men in white coats finally convinced me it was 2047. This made it hard to speak, but I was too curious to not ask questions. "And what part is that?"

"New York. Actually, they took over a lot more than New York, but that's where we are. Listen, I was hoping to break this to you gently, but you were so insistent about getting answers. The reason you don't see any nurses or in-room dining or *windows* is this is not a hospital. This is a research facility run by the Chinese. And you, I suppose, *are* their lab rat."

"How in the hell did China take over the country? We have the number one military in the world."

"*Had* the number one military. Though, it was more than a matter of military might."

Alex's gaze drifted to the wall behind me. When he continued speaking, his voice took on a tinge of pain. "They took advantage of us in our darkest hour. The Cumbre Vieja started it all. Have you heard of it?"

I shook my head.

"Cumbre Vieja was a volcanic fissure that ran across La Palma island in the Canaries. They are located off the northwest coast of Africa."

"I know the Canaries. Been there twice, actually. Surf is really good. Never did much sightseeing, though. Spent all my time in the water."

"You could have seen what started all of this mess," Alex said, gesturing to our surroundings. "The experts knew Cumbre Vieja was a threat. The fissure was filled with steam and molten rock. There was so little holding the two halves of the island together that the entire western flank would drop by ten or twenty feet whenever there was an eruption. Still, geologists said it would take ten thousand years for the fissure to reach critical mass. But then on January thirteenth in twenty thirty-six it happened. The eruption was massive. It ripped the island apart at the fissure, and the entire western flank crashed into the sea. It was a piece of land thirteen miles long, ten miles wide, and more than a mile thick. Five hundred billion tons of earth."

"Holy shit, man. That's like an asteroid hit the Earth."

"As close as you can get. When the waves started, they were three thousand feet high. They were so powerful that they wiped every single structure from the Canaries beneath the high water mark."

"Those poor people. They didn't even have a chance."

"The casualties at the epicenter were infinitesimal compared to the rest of the world. The waves were still a hundred and eighty feet high when they reached the US. They demolished the entire Eastern seaboard from Maine to Miami."

"Not the people, though, right? Tell me they had time to evacuate."

"Yes, they tried. People in the Southeast did all right. Though, I suppose that's a relative term. The eruption happened in the middle of our night. The devastation in the Canaries was so complete that we weren't even notified until the waves reached Morocco, which was more than an hour after the eruption. Once NOAA pieced things together, they kicked evacuations into high gear. Officials were going street-by-street, rousing people from their sleep. Still, they had enough time for that. That wasn't the issue. The real problem was how people reacted. They acted like a hurricane was coming. People boarded up their homes before they left, for God's sake!"

I buried my face in my hands.

"When the waves hit at daybreak traffic was a snarled mess on roads out of coastal areas. This probably would have been all right for the size waves they were expecting. I suppose you could say human error played a role here as well. Do you know how a tsunami is detected?"

"Do they still use those buoys anchored to the sea floor?"

"Yes, the buoys measure wave height and pressure via a sensor anchored to the sea floor. The waves were so large that the buoys were ripped from their moorings. The data they sent to the satellites was absolute garbage. Then you had this anecdotal stuff coming in from areas the waves had reached and it was hard to believe, let alone understand. It was off the charts. When a fifty-foot wave moves into a coastal area, people can see it and observe its height. It will hit a building and, as long as it doesn't destroy it, people can tell you the wave's height based on what floor it reaches. But when a two- or three-thousand foot wave reaches the coastline it just obliterates it. The waves in North Africa and Western Europe carved a path of destruction that stretched a hundred and fifty miles inland in places. You had people who lived in the mountains a good two-hour drive from the coast reporting the high water mark at their doorstep. How do you calculate wave height from that?"

"You can't."

"Not in the miniscule amount of time they had to work with. We had the greatest atmospheric scientists in the world working to determine what was headed our way, and they were handicapped. They were working blind. Human nature took over. They worked from the models they knew, and none of these models understood that a hundred and eighty foot wave could reach the East Coast."

"So the people sitting in traffic were . . ."

"The waves reached seventeen miles inland in low-lying areas. They say a million vehicles were swept from the roadways in Florida alone."

"That's sickening."

"I wish it was the worst of it. Up here, we were in the midst of a massive nor'easter. Blizzard conditions stretched from Maine down into northern Virginia. The heavy snowfall and lack of visibility choked the roadways. People knew the waves were bearing down on them, but there was nowhere to go. They were trapped."

Tears welled in Alex's eyes as he spoke.

"How many people died?"

"No one knows for sure. Ten million were living on Long Island alone, and the waves washed right over it and into the Sound. A very small fraction of coastal residents made it far enough inland. The bitter cold severely limited the chance of survival for the masses caught in the barrage of water. There was never a final death count because we soon faced an even greater problem."

"The Chinese?"

"Yes."

"Don't tell me they just came barreling in right behind the waves."

"No, we let them in."

"What do you mean?"

"You have to realize, the tsunami created a crisis of gargantuan proportions. It was—"

"Biblical."

"Yes, indeed. From top to bottom, the East Coast looked like it had been littered with nuclear bombs. The disaster was more than our country—any country—was prepared to handle. There were massive throngs of displaced citizens who needed food and shelter. And the impact area—the impact area was beyond comprehension. The dead outnumbered the living by a wide margin, and still, there were more survivors scattered among the debris than rescue personnel."

"So we let them in to help?"

"Yes, their offer appeared genuine and most generous. China is not the country you knew. Their economy dwarfed ours long before the tsunami hit. They had tamed inflation, overpopulation . . . even their massive appetite for natural resources wasn't able to hold them back. China had become the world's premier superpower, and they acted the part. Aiding other countries in need was their imperialistic duty, just as it had been ours for so many years."

I dropped the chopsticks onto my plate with a loud ping. I'd wiped the plate clean while listening to Alex and wasn't sure what to do with it. The plate and chopsticks were made of ceramic that didn't seem disposable. Alex walked the plate and chopsticks over to the vending machine and slid them into a slot. The machine whined as they were cleaned somewhere deep within its hull. Alex continued speaking.

"A bustling economy provided ample means to grow their military, and they went about it aggressively. They built a massive naval fleet complete with aircraft carriers, a modern air force, and ten *million* troops. They even landed men on Mars, for Pete's sake. It was a clear case of the apprentice becoming the master. It is quite interesting to look back now because, initially, the growth of their military created so much anxiety in this country. We worried about their intentions. But things calmed down when it seemed they just wanted to get their chips in the game that we had created. Just like us, they began *liberating* countries from oppressive regimes in order to get their hands on oil and other natural resources. It got to the point that things were downright harmonious, at least for the game being played. There were far more countries in need of *liberating* than a single superpower could handle. So, rather than fighting over them, they were divvied up somehow. This was never spoken of publicly, but you had to wonder when you had China intervening here and we were there and there was very little acrimony involved. The two bullies were never on the same block."

"They must have been considered a threat."

"A threat? Yes. Threatening? No. Thus, their offer of assistance was taken at face value. Relations between our countries were strong enough that Chinese aid was logical and appreciated. Besides, we were in desperate shape. Beggars do not have the luxury of choice."

"Instead they just came in with guns blazing?"

"No, not at all. That would have been easier to defend against. The first wave of the Chinese fleet anchored off the East Coast just days after the tsunami. From there they set up land operations up and down the coast. Most of their efforts were dedicated to search and rescue, which was what we needed most. Food was easy enough to bring in from the West for the refugees. The whole country rallied to help. It was a beautiful thing to see. But the search and rescue operation was too massive to do alone. And the debris made land access to coastal areas difficult. The vast majority of vessels in the North and Central Atlantic, including major components of our Atlantic fleet, were sunk or marooned by the waves. That meant the Chinese ships were among the first to arrive. They were right behind the activated elements of our Pacific fleet. And there were *a lot* of them."

"Why did we lose so many ships? You'd think they'd just send them out to deeper water to weather the waves."

"In some cases that worked, but for the most part the waves defied logic. We lost a carrier group on the open ocean that was cruising near the Canaries when Cumbre Vieja fell. They don't build ships to withstand waves three thousand feet high. Back here with the nor'easter hindering land evacuations the government decided to load people onto ships and evacuate them that way. This took a while to orchestrate and once the ships were loaded there was little time for them to head out into deeper water. They thought they were going to be deep enough, but, like I said, the size of the oncoming waves was grossly underestimated."

"My God, they thought they were being rescued and the ships sank?"

"Yes, the waves caused many, many tragedies, and the sunken ships helped open the door to a significant Chinese presence on our shores. We no longer had enough vessels to cover two thousand miles of shoreline. I suppose they could have brought every remaining vessel to the East Coast, but that would have been foolish, even in a crisis like this. Thank goodness, they kept a naval presence on the West Coast. If they hadn't, the Chinese would have taken over the entire country."

"How so?"

"Well, the war began just weeks after the tsunami. By that point, the Chinese had a significant number of men on the ground helping with the rescue and recovery effort. But it still wasn't enough. They offered a second fleet to join the effort, and it was absolutely massive. A few days after it arrived, they made it clear that helping us was the last thing they wanted. The strike was so carefully orchestrated, so elegant in design, that the Chinese must have been planning it since the day the tsunami struck. They had but one opportunity to use the element of surprise, and they made sure it was a crushing blow. First, they launched missiles that took out our satellites. Then they unleashed the firepower of their floating armada to sink our ships and hobble military installations in the East. Their forces on the ground were another major component of the coordinated assault. They had secretly stockpiled weapons and machinery among their supplies for the rescue operation. They had worked for weeks right alongside our troops—troops that were not equipped for battle. Sure, they had rifles, but they were not there to fight. When the Chinese troops on the ground attacked, it was a slaughter. They attacked soldiers who were—at best—lightly armed. When our troops tried to regroup and assemble, they had no GPS and no space-based imagery of the enemy's movements. With their main operating bases getting hammered from the sea and the air, they were cut off . . . isolated. It was not a fair fight."

"The Chinese aid was just a Trojan horse."

"Yes."

"The Chinese must not have gone far. I mean, there's a lot of firepower out West. They must've come in and shut 'em down."

"They weren't able to. At least not initially."

"Why the hell not?"

"The Chinese attacked the West Coast simultaneously. Some people think it was a red herring; that they just wanted to split our forces and didn't plan on winning the West. I believe they tried to take both coasts. They were so high on power . . . so greedy. Plus, our forces were already spread thin when the tsunami struck. We had a massive number of troops fighting conflicts in the Middle East and North Africa. When the tsunami hit, we couldn't just pick them up and bring them home on a moment's notice. The Chinese knew that, and they took advantage of it while they could. But they failed to anticipate how hard we were willing to fight to defend our homeland. It took just five months to quell the attack in the West. The Chinese fleet retreated from the West Coast, and we sent more troops to the eastern front. This slowed their progress considerably and eventually led to a stalemate along the Mississippi. To this day, that's where the front remains. It has been almost ten years since either side has gained significant ground on either side of the Mississippi."

I slid my chair away from the table. The problems of US citizens of the future were becoming my problems. I was no longer just a lab rat for the Chinese. I was a lab rat for the Chinese trapped a thousand miles behind enemy lines. Finding my wife and son felt impossible. I leaned forward with my elbow on my knee and pushed my thumb and index fingers into my forehead until the pressure spread them apart.

"That's just . . ." I searched the room. "It's fucked is what it is. They took control of *everything* east of the Mississippi?"

"Yes."

"They took over Chicago?"

"They did."

"Miami?"

"Yes."

"Philly?"

"Yes."

"Birmingham?"

"Yes," Alex answered with growing exasperation. "The Chinese control absolutely everything east of the Mississippi. They even renamed cities."

"What about our allies? Didn't they come and help?"

"Some of our best allies were more devastated by the tsunami than we were. The exposed coasts of France, Spain, and Portugal were wiped clean. Great Britain as well; they were much closer to the epicenter. I suppose they would have sent forces after hearing of the attack, but the Chinese sent *aid missions* to them as well."

"Those bastards did the Trojan horse thing to them, too?"

"Yes, and the NATO countries unaffected by the tsunami sent their troops to fight the war in Europe. They were not willing to send them across the Atlantic when the enemy was knocking on their door. The Canadian military provided some assistance."

"Phbbt! Some help they must have been if the Chinese took half the friggin' country." I was fuming. I stood up from the table and went back to pacing.

Alex looked uncomfortable. "Well, they have helped us where it helps them," he said meekly. "They sent forces down early in the war to help stabilize the front, and we couldn't have done it without them. Who knows how far west the Chinese would have gone? The Canadians are unwilling to stage a full-scale invasion. They feel that doing so poses too great a risk. They would be defenseless if it failed. So they maintain their border, and they will help us take back the rest of our country when the time is right."

"You really buy that crap, Al? How many years has it been? How many years since they lent a hand to their next-door neighbor?"

This was the first question I'd asked that Alex actually had to think about before he could answer. "It has been six, no seven, umm . . . it has been more than eight years since their forces returned home."

"Now, Al, do you really believe they are going to wake up one day and say, 'You know what guys? Let's get back down there and help the Americans take back their land. We don't want their children to have to live their lives without knowing what freedom feels like."

Alex stared at me submissively. "No, I suppose not."

"You're damn right they're not. Old Rip Van Winkle here may be behind the eight ball, but at least I know bullshit when I see it."

Alex stood up and took a step toward the hallway. "We should make our way back to your room. I'm supposed to be helping you to get back on your feet. They're going to question why we've been in here so long."

I placed a firm hand on Alex's shoulder. "Hold on a minute. You said I was the first *successful* reanimation. Are you saying they tried on some other saps and it didn't work?"

"We really should be moving along."

"We can talk about it here, or we can talk about it in front of them. It's your call."

Alex stepped back reluctantly. He spoke nervously, looking over my shoulder as he spoke. "Yes, there were others before you, none of which were successful. They had a breakthrough on your case. Now they believe they can successfully reanimate all of the other cryonics stored here. You're going to have company."

"Company?"

"Today, in fact. They are reanimating several cryonics right now who are going to be joining you once they are stabilized."

"Are any of them Ted Williams?"

"I'm afraid not."

"You know Ted Williams?"

"Of course I do. He's the greatest hitter of all time."

At least something was right with the world.

"You know, Al, the thing I don't understand is why the Chinese even care about this business of bringing frozen people back to life. Why does it matter?"

"They need more troops."

I swallowed. Alex smiled. "No, not you. They want to freeze soldiers who die in battle. This way, they can send them back to base to have them treated and reanimated. It will allow them to fix a person just like they would a tank. Think about it. Soldiers are scarce commodities when you're fighting wars on three continents."

"Wow. Just like putting another quarter into a video game."

"Like what?"

"Oh, nothing."

"We really do need to go."

"Hold your horses, Al. Just one more question."

"All right, just please make it quick."

"Where do you stand in all this?"

"Where do I stand in all of what?" he spat.

It was curious Alex was such a knowledgeable and compliant participant in a Chinese lab. His petulance at my question amplified my suspicion. I leaned forward carefully and spoke with accentuated base, "Well, Al, seems to me you are well versed in the interests and activities of the Chinese. And here you are, in their lab, helping them with their little science project. So, I need to know what your deal is. What kind of traitor are you?"

Alex sighed deeply before he spoke, "I am not any kind." Then he stood up and worked his way toward the hallway, speaking hurriedly while motioning for me to follow.

"Things are far more complicated now than when you were alive. You'll fare better once you can settle on that fact. And you'd be wise to trust me. I seriously doubt you'll find a better option."

5.

Alex led me down the hallway past my room. I figured he was just taking me out to stretch my legs. Then we turned the corner at the end of the corridor. The hallway stopped in front of a massive observation room. We stood before the oversized pane of glass and watched the busy operation on the other side. The men in white coats were hard at work. They gathered at stations with corpses in various stages of reanimation. It was an assembly line, of sorts, but instead of widgets, they were making people.

On the left side of the room, a row of tall silver canisters like oversized water heaters had been polished to a reflective sheen. A sticker affixed to the side of each canister read: CAUTION. BIOMATERIAL. KEEP BELOW -150° CELSIUS AT ALL TIMES. It gave me the chills to think that I had been frozen inside one of those gleaming, silver tubes just days before.

Two of the Chinese scientists approached the canister closest to us. They wrestled the lid off, and vapor hissed. The scientists maneuvered a small crane that looked an awful lot like an engine hoist above the cylinder. The crane had a rubberized metallic claw that reached down into the cylinder and retrieved the wrinkled, frozen corpse. They maneuvered her gingerly with the claw, like a child retrieving a stuffed animal from a machine. She looked more like an extra-terrestrial than a person. Her shriveled skin pulled taut against her bony frame, and her face was mummified in a fixed, lifeless expression. Vapor emanated from her body. They placed her in a specialized incubator. Alex explained that it would thaw her flesh in preparation for the next stage of the process. God himself couldn't breathe life into something so wretched, but the men in white coats were doing it all over the room, right before our eyes.

Three scientists worked on a freshly defrosted man lying on a gurney. His skin was so moist it was weeping. The woman next to him was further along in the process. Scientists were transplanting a heart. So many men in white coats surrounded the body on the far right that I could only see the bottoms of gangly male feet. This one at least looked like a person. The skin was plump and firm, albeit pale. I spotted the man in charge shouting orders at the others. Tubes snaked out in all directions, and a trio of refrigerator-sized machines dutifully thumped away behind the scientists.

And then I heard it—the same violent screaming I had succumbed to upon being reanimated. The twisted feet started shaking and writhing in agony. The screams grew louder and more primal. Smiling widely, the man in charge observed the patient carefully and then ordered the men in white coats to sedate him. The screaming finally stopped.

"Are you feeling all right?" Alex asked.

His question pulled me out of the room. Once again, I saw the glass in front of me.

"Um, I think so. Why?"

"You're sweating."

Beads of perspiration had collected on my forehead, and my collar was soaked. I hadn't even noticed. I wiped my hand across my forehead, and the sweat dripped down my palm onto the linoleum. I began feeling light headed.

"Yeah, I . . . I guess this was a little much."

"Too soon? I'm sorry. I thought it would help. I should have realized."

"It's OK, Al."

We turned and walked back toward my room. When we returned to the room, I was actually happy to lie down on that cardboard bed. Thinking about the shriveled skin, the canisters, the twitching feet, the screaming, I started sweating again. To put it out of my mind, I thought of Colt. I pictured him living on the beach in San Diego with a beautiful wife and family. I imagined a little boy toddling around them who looked just like my boy did when he was in diapers. Hope that he was still alive was the only thing that put my mind at ease enough to sleep.

6.

The beep of the door woke me up. The lights turned on, and through cracked eyelids, I saw white lab coats scurrying back and forth. I sat up and rubbed my eyes. I felt groggy and heavy, like I'd overslept. Two orderlies supervised by a man in a white coat wheeled in a guy on a bed. The man in the bed was sleeping, and they positioned him next to some machinery and left the room. He looked like hell. Not because of being frozen, at least as far as I could tell, but because he was decrepit. He looked to me about seventy, but like he'd either had some serious illnesses later in life, lived hard prior, or probably both. Watching him breathing there in his bed—all wrinkled and frail—I wondered why he had bothered to get frozen at all. Even the mad Chinese scientists were only going to be able to squeeze a couple more years out of him.

Next they brought in a much younger woman that couldn't have been more than forty. She looked pretty healthy and a bit plump. Her skin was firm, she had a smooth complexion, and her large bosom overflowed under her gown. I wondered what she had died of. I could come up with a laundry list of possibilities for the grandpa lying in the bed next to hers, but she was a toughie. I didn't have much time to ponder the possibilities before our final companion was wheeled in. I realize a man who lives in a glass house shouldn't throw stones, but this guy was a heart attack for certain. Restora must have customized an extra-large cryogenic container for him because he looked like a beached whale on that gurney. I couldn't gauge his age from across the room because his enormous belly obscured his face.

The orderlies and men in white coats left the room. It was just us cryonics. I sat on my bed and watched nervously while they slept. It surprised me how I longed for their companionship. I felt like a boy again, waiting impatiently outside my teenage brother's room for him to wake up. Here were some people that were just like me—my fellow lab rats. They would get my jokes. They would be shocked and furious to find out what happened to the world, and together we would find a way out.

One by one, the butterflies emerged from their cocoons. Each one looked around the room, confused and sedated. Then they smiled when they saw me, and started chatting. Barry was the first to wake up. Boy, did he have some stories to tell. Barry was the frail gentleman I'd thought was in his seventies. Turns out he was only in his early sixties when he died. Barry was the only child of a heavy-drinking oil tycoon who succumbed to alcoholism at an early age. That left Barry a trust fund baby, and he sure would've made Papa proud. Every moment of his life was spent drinking, doing drugs, and chasing women. He had died just twelve years ago. Barry signed up for cryonics when alcoholism had taken its toll and he knew he didn't have much time left. Medicine at the time Barry was dying could treat alcoholism easily. Organ farms produced petri dish livers and whatever you needed replaced, unless you were an alcoholic. A conservative movement in the government banned organ transplants for alcoholics. So, Barry found a loophole. The research at the time suggested they'd be reanimating cryonics in a hundred years' time. Barry was shocked to find himself alive and rebuilt a little more than a decade after kicking the bucket.

Elliott awoke next. It wasn't five minutes before he and Barry were carrying on like a couple of frat boys. Elliott was an investment banker born in nineteen eighty-one. He'd amassed great wealth by running a large brokerage house through what he and Barry called "the greatest bull market in history" during the "roaring twenties." Elliott was so into cryonics that he had set aside investments carefully selected to mature in the long term. He figured once he was reanimated, and people knew cryonics worked, they'd be signing up for it in droves. So, Elliott planned on building a cryonic estate planning business. He'd help people build an investment portfolio that would serve their needs from the great beyond. Upon reanimation, his clients would be far wealthier than when they died. Elliott didn't die of a heart attack. By the time he died in twenty thirty-five, heart attacks had been all but eradicated by non-invasive laser cleaning of the circulatory system. So, he was a glutton most of his adult life with little consequence. Elliott did have trouble sleeping, though, and he was pretty sure he kicked the bucket by drowning in a pool while on sleeping pills. At least that's the last thing he remembered.

By the time Janet joined the fray, we had a regular party going. The youngest of the group, Janet died in twenty thirty-one at the age of thirty-eight. She'd worked as a chief nursing officer for a hospital system, and had signed up for cryonics because she wanted to see the future of medicine. Janet was visibly disappointed when I told them it was twenty forty-seven. I suppose the people at Restora who figured reanimation would be possible at the end of the century didn't count on the Chinese military developing the technology half a century sooner.

Janet was such a nice lady—a real spark plug. She got over her disappointment pretty quickly. And why shouldn't she? She had a second chance at life and didn't know she was a prisoner of the Chinese military. The three of them were all so happy to be alive. I couldn't spoil that. When they asked about the world, I told them I'd just been reanimated myself and didn't know much. I figured they'd have plenty of time for despair. Plus, I hated being a buzz kill. Lord knows Alex was plenty good at that. He'd be in soon enough to set them straight.

Or so I thought. No one came back to our room until people started getting sick. Elliott came down with it first. It was that same evening, a little while after we'd all fallen asleep. Elliott was moaning so loudly we all woke up. He said his arms and legs ached terribly. The machines near the bed must have sent data to the men in white coats because a couple of them came into the room shortly thereafter. They dismissed Elliott's pain as a side effect of being reanimated. Those two were clearly the incompetent members of the bunch. They didn't even bother to take a good look at him. The other men in white coats were probably too busy scheming how to make frozen soldiers to pay Elliott any attention.

The side effect explanation calmed Elliott down. We reminded him of the horrible burning sensation we all experienced upon being reanimated and postulated he was having some sort of after-effect from that. I lay awake for a couple of hours. In time, Elliott's grunts and groans subsided, and Janet and Barry fell asleep. I didn't see how I could possibly rally those three to rise against the Chinese. They seemed too complacent, too slow to question. I hoped Alex breaking the bad news to them would provide enough motivation to buck authority.

7.

I was still lying there thinking when the tootling started. It was the oddest sound. Definitely not something I would associate with an alarm. I sat up in bed, and the lights in the room turned on. The noise was coming from the machinery near Elliott's bed. I rushed over. He'd taken a turn for the worse. He was barely conscious and sweating. His skin was puffed and clammy.

A man in a white coat came in robotically, unconcerned by the alarm. As soon as he saw Elliott draped across the bed like a wet rag, he did an immediate one eighty and headed out the door. He came back with the entire team of lemmings who rushed into the room behind the man in charge. He pulled the body-scanning device from his pocket, and it projected a hologram of Elliott. I looked over at Barry with a raised brow, hoping to recycle my *Star Wars* joke, but the grave look on his face shut me down. I felt bad for wanting to goof around while Elliott was gravely ill, but I knew the men in charge were about to work some magic on him. As the hologram scrolled through various perspectives of Elliott's innards, the men in white coats pensively grunted and pointed.

True to form, the man in charge shouted instructions at one of his minions who left the room and returned with a large metal pen. The man in charge took the pen and placed it against the side of Elliott's neck. It made a loud popping sound like the flashbulb of an old-fashioned camera. He looked at Elliott's face and grunted with self-approval. Then he tried to leave the room.

"Is Elliott going to be all right?" Barry asked.

The man in charge paused in the doorway and spun around on one leg to face Barry. "Mister Elliott has a viral infection."

"What kind of virus?" Barry prodded.

"It is nothing for you to be concerned about. We can cure any virus quickly. You will see very soon."

"But what does he have? He seems very sick—" Janet chimed in.

"No more questions!" the man in charge roared. He turned and left the room.

"He sure is a barrel of laughs," Barry quipped.

"You ought to see him when he's really pissed."

"Who is he?" Janet asked.

"Look guys, it's a long story. I mean, we can get some information in the morning. Let's get some rest. I'm sure Elliott will be fine."

8.

Later that evening Barry and Janet fell ill. At first I could hear them writhing in their beds, breathing heavily through their noses. Then they started moaning and grunting just like Elliott had.

One of the men in the white coats returned and gave them each a shot in the neck. He didn't speak any English so I couldn't get any answers out of him.

Being stuck in a room with three violently ill people made me antsy. I may not have had much to live for, but something visceral kicked in, a survival instinct if you will. It made me want to get the hell out of there.

I knew the door was locked, as it had been since my arrival. It always opened for Alex and the men in white coats without any discernible effort. I groped the walls and crawled across the floor in vain, hoping to find an activation switch. I got back into my bed, which suddenly felt like it was made of stone. I listened to them squirming beneath their sheets. Sleep was out of the question. I was trapped.

9.

Alex arrived first thing in the morning. He must have thought I was still asleep because he went right to his work. I sat up and tried to attract his attention, but he ignored me. "Al, hey Al." Nothing. He had his back to me and tinkered away on the dials. He didn't seem concerned that I was living in a leper colony. "Alex!"

Alex looked over his shoulder. "Oh, good morning, Royce."

"Where were you last night?"

"Me? I don't sleep here."

"Listen, Al, you gotta tell me what's going on with these people. They're dropping like flies in here."

"I don't want to scare you, but they're not entirely certain. They should be coming in shortly to have a look. Perhaps Dr. Feng will give you an update."

"Dr. Feng?"

"He's the lead physician on the cryonics team."

"The asshole?"

"Right. I have to run." Alex headed out the door.

I looked across the room at my three companions. They lay on their backs in their beds in dead silence. I could see Janet and Barry's abdomens rising with each breath, but Elliott's was not. I stepped slowly toward Elliott's bed to have a look. Elliott looked hideous. His vapid skin had a charcoal gray undertone punctuated by black hemorrhagic blotches. His throat was covered with large blistering sores. Some oozed a milky fluid that trickled down his neck. His eyes were closed, and I couldn't hear him breathing. I was afraid he was dead. I moved in closer to see if he was breathing. I turned my head so my ear was beside Elliott's mouth and I could look up at the rest of his face. I felt a gentle burst of cold air from Elliott's nose. At least he was alive.

His eyelids lifted slowly, revealing deep crimson orbs. I jumped back from the bed. The whites of his eyes were filled with blood. Elliott didn't react. I don't think he even knew I was there. He just stared at the ceiling, motionless. I stood there breathing heavily, chuckling to myself for having been so squeamish.

Barry and Janet weren't looking much better. Their skin had begun taking on the charcoal tone, and fresh volcanic sores erupted from their necks. While I stood there looking at the three of them, I felt alone. My new companions were not going to make it. There would be no mutiny. No cryonic uprising. It was just me against the world, once again.

10.

I was thrilled when Dr. Feng finally barged into the room. If there was any hope for them, he was it. The doctors poked and prodded the sick. For more than an hour, they debated and obsessed over the imagery produced by their holograms.

Alex came in next holding a cherry red instrument the size of a soda can. He handed the device to Dr. Feng who used it to generate a hologram of Elliott's brain. The men in the white coats oohd and ahhd at the image projected. To me it looked like any other brain. Dr. Feng frowned and sat down on the edge of Elliott's bed.

Alex worked his way over toward me.

"What's happening?"

At first he spoke under his breath and feigned checking on my machines. "They are really, really sick. The doctors don't know how to stop it."

"Thanks, genius. You don't need grad school to see that."

Ambushed yet again by my sarcasm, Alex whipped his head in my direction.

"It's something they've never seen before. Some sort of variola virus."

"Tell Feng to give them some antibiotics."

Alex rolled his eyes. He looked over his shoulder. The men in the white coats were too focused on their work to pay us any attention. He loosened up a little.

"Are you serious?"

"Sorry, *doctor*."

"Look, this is something very serious. Shhh, shhh, hold on a second—" Alex paused.

"You speak Chinese?" I whispered, as if that would somehow allow him to listen to me and still hear them.

"Shhhhh! Just a minute. Let me listen." Alex hung on their every word. "The virus is eating away at their brains. It has specialized prions that are selectively destroying the areas responsible for higher-order thinking."

"What does that mean?"

"It means the lights are on, but nobody is home."

"How did you pick all that up?"

"It's what the doctors are saying."

"You speak Chinese?"

"Of course I speak Chinese. I've been living under their rule for ten years. If you don't pick it up, you don't do so well around here. Wait a minute, something else is going on."

The men in white coats were gathered around Elliott, and two were locked in an intense argument. They called Alex over. He fiddled with the dials on the machine and explained something to the group. The entire group began debating. Alex slipped out from the middle of the fracas and came back over to me.

"What is that all about?"

"His oxygen levels are so low that they thought something was wrong with the machine. I've never seen anything like it. I can't believe he isn't—" A long shrill beep from the same machine interrupted him.

It was a sound I'd heard before. Elliott was flatlining. The men in white coats panicked. They tried desperately to revive him, but it was no use. Then Janet's machine went off. The entire team save two men ran to her bedside. They weren't working on Janet for two minutes when Barry's machine went off. Half the men at Janet's bedside ran to work on Barry. It was complete chaos.

Alex ran over to help with Barry, though he kind of just muddled about waiting for instructions from the men in white coats. The doctors gave up trying to revive Elliot and joined the efforts at reviving Barry and Janet. Several minutes passed while I sat in my bed watching the bedlam. I was mostly watching the men in white coats working on Barry. His bed was adjacent to Elliott's, and it looked like they were going to give up on him as well. That's when I noticed something moving in my periphery. Elliott's arm rose slowly from the mattress

"Hey look, look, he's still alive!" I yelled across the room. I pointed and gestured maniacally in Elliott's direction. No one paid me any attention.

The same arm reached over and grabbed hold of one of the men in white coats. Elliott pulled the man backwards until he fell on top of him and then he wrapped his other arm around the man and held him tight. Once Elliott had a good hold on him, he took a vicious bite out of the man's neck. I ran over to Elliott's bed on instinct, more for Elliott's sake than anything. If he wanted to maul our captors, that was fine with me, I just wanted to make sure they didn't retaliate.

The doctors ran to their colleague's aid. He screamed and flailed, kicking his legs in the air as he struggled to break free from Elliott's grasp. Blood came gushing forth from his jugular in rhythmic pulses, splashing on the men's lab coats. As soon as they got the victim loose, they held Elliott down and activated the restraint system, which held Elliott firmly in place. Alex froze in horror.

Elliott looked mental. A thick glaze dulled his eyes, and his pupils were hyper-dilated. He was taking hurried shallow breaths, and strained to lift his head as high off the mattress as the restraints would allow. Saliva gathered around the perimeter of his mouth, and anytime someone came near he groaned at them and gnashed his teeth.

"You! Back to your bed!" Dr. Feng barked. He pointed toward my bed.

When I didn't move quickly enough, he and the other doctors grabbed me by the arms and pulled me down onto the mattress. Dr. Feng stomped on the pedal that activated my restraints.

"Perhaps now you'll stay where you belong," Dr. Feng hissed.

Dr. Feng ordered two of the men in white coats to take Elliott's victim away for treatment. Janet and Barry lay there just as they had before, silent and unresponsive. Dr. Feng observed Barry closely. He searched for a pulse and pried his eyelids open to check his pupils with a flashlight.

"They're dead, genius," I jeered. "You and your machines took great care of them. Way to go."

Dr. Feng didn't even look in my direction. He studied every inch of Barry. The instant Barry opened his erubescent eyes, Dr. Feng restrained him. A moment later, Barry was moaning and snapping his teeth at Dr. Feng.

Feng pointed and yelled to his colleagues at Janet's bedside, imploring them to restrain her before she reanimated. As he held his arm out above Barry, the sagging sleeve of his loose lab coat dangled just within Barry's reach. He craned his neck and bit down tight on Feng's sleeve. Once he got a hold of the sleeve, Barry snapped his neck back so hard it pinned Feng's shoulder to the mattress.

Feng propped a foot up against the bed and used it along with his free hand to push against Barry's grasp. Their tug of war swayed back and forth until the sleeve tore free from the lab coat, flinging Feng backwards into the metal frame on the side of Elliott's bed. He slumped to the floor in a heap, his derriere landing right on the pedal that controlled the restraint system. The restraints retracted, and Elliott sprang into action. He chomped down hard on Feng's shoulder. Feng shrieked and pulled away. A jagged chunk of flesh tore free from Feng's shoulder and hung limply from Elliott's mouth.

Dr. Feng scrambled to his feet and backed away from Elliott in a panic. When he turned and ran out the door, Elliott lumbered off after him. The remaining men in white coats left Janet's bedside and gave chase down the hall and out of sight, save one who was caught by Janet's arm and dragged to the ground. The men in white coats had been too distracted to restrain Janet. She was still during Feng's episode, but came to life just in time to grab the doctor's leg as he bumped into her on his way out. Janet hung on tight to the man in the white coat. He kept on running, pulling her out of the bed and onto the floor. She got a hold of his foot with her other hand and pulled him down. She flipped him onto his back, held his arms down with her legs, and proceeded to devour his face and neck. His desperate cries were choked with blood. It wasn't long before they stopped. Janet kept on eating, pulling and tearing at the flesh with her mouth and hands.

Alex stood petrified in the corner of the room. I heard bones crunching while Janet tore into the man in the white coat. I didn't know why the other cryonics became homicidal cannibals, but I knew if I stayed strapped in that bed I'd be on the menu.

"Al," I said just loud enough for him to hear. I was trying not to draw Janet's attention, since she was positioned between Alex and me. I motioned with my head for Alex to come over. He shook his head.

"Get over here!" I yelled through gritted teeth. Janet didn't even look up. Neither did Alex. He stared at his feet like a child.

"Are you just going to let her eat us?" I struggled against the straps.

Alex looked like he might cry.

"Well, are you?"

He didn't even look up.

"Come on, now . . . grow a pair!" My volume made Alex nervous. He placed an index finger across his lips, pleading with me to keep quiet. "Oh, oh, I see! You want to watch her eat me, don't you?" I screamed.

Alex trembled and shook. Tears welled up in his eyes, and he clasped his hands together, pleading with me to stop.

"Jaanet, ooooh Jaaanet . . . come and get me, Janet!" I screamed at the top of my lungs. "Big Al wants to watch you rip me apart!"

Alex started shuffling anxiously along the perimeter of the room like his shoelaces were tied together. He fixed his gaze on the floor, save an occasional peek in Janet's direction. She paid him no mind. When Alex reached the middle of the room and was nearest to Janet, he was forced to maneuver around a large machine. This pushed his path even further in Janet's direction. When Alex came near, she stopped eating for a moment to glare—a lioness guarding a fresh kill. Alex closed his eyes and kept on shuffling, opening them only when the restraint release pedal was within reach.

As soon as the straps were off, I ran toward the door. Alex opened it, and we shot through the door into the hallway. The hallway was empty and quiet, just as every other time I'd been in it. But this time there were bloody footprints stamped along the corridor floor.

11.

"What now?" I asked.

"Um, we need to get out of here before they quarantine the building. They'll seal it off, and we don't want to be inside."

"Won't they come looking for us?"

"Probably. Depends on how long it takes to clean up this mess."

"Hold this open for me." I cracked the door to the room and peeked inside. Janet was still on the floor, gorging on the man in the white coat.

Alex hugged my waist and tried to yank me back into the hallway. "What are you doing?" he grunted.

"Just keep the door open. I'll be right back."

I wriggled free from Alex and tiptoed into the room, making my way toward Barry's bed. He was still a rabid dog, growling and biting at the air, spittle flinging from his mouth. I surveyed my surroundings for something long and settled on an IV stand. I loosened the knob on the side of the stand and extended the pole as far as it would slide. I tightened the knob and held the stand out above the release pedal for Barry's restraints. I paused to judge the distance. I figured I had roughly a seven-foot head start on a horse that was going to be quick out the gates. I took a deep breath and let go of the stand, turning for the door before it hit the ground. As I dashed for the door I could hear the whine of the retreating straps and could feel Barry's clumsy feet stomping on the linoleum. Alex held the door as requested and I slipped through the crack, turned, and slammed it shut. I could hear pounding on the other side of the door that sounded like more than one person. I must have riled them both up. When I peered through the observation window, I saw Barry and Janet pounding on the door and running into it like a couple of mental patients.

"What was that for?" Alex was furious.

"Just making a bigger mess," I said with a smile.

"All right, let's go. I know a way out."

We ducked through a door just down the hallway from my room. On the other side was a concrete stairwell. It was cool and a bit damp in there. I heard screaming and banging on the floor above us, haunting sounds that seeped through the walls and echoed within the concrete passageway. We ran down three flights of stairs before we reached the ground floor. Alex cracked the door, and we peered outside. It was a marble-floored lobby, and daylight shone through the glass doors of the building's entrance just ten paces to our left. Two macabre figures in orange hazmat suits waddled through the front door. We pulled the door tight as they made their way past us.

Alex cracked the door again and peeked out.

"You see anybody?"

"No, it's clear."

"Let's run for it."

Alex swung the door open, and we ran for the entrance. We opened the building's glass entrance doors and stepped outside where we were greeted by the hissing of air brakes. I grabbed Alex and pulled him over a short cement wall that ran perpendicular to the edge of the building's façade. A large black personnel carrier climbed the curb and parked against the building's steps. A dozen soldiers leapt from the back of the truck and sprinted toward the entrance, forming a human blockade in front of the doors.

We hid and sat with our backs against the wall.

"We need to get out of here, now," Alex whispered.

"Shouldn't we wait until those soldiers leave?"

"They won't. As soon as reinforcements arrive, they'll set up a perimeter around the entire building while the hazmat crews work inside. No one gets in or out."

"And if they catch us?"

"We're the exception. They'll put us back in there until the quarantine is lifted."

Images of bloody teeth and fiery eyes flooded my mind. There was no way the soldiers were getting me back inside that building alive. "Well, what the hell are we gonna do? We can't just run for it. They'll see us."

With nowhere to go, we exchanged nervous glances between looks over the wall's edge. I could hear the roar of truck engines approaching from down the block. We were sitting ducks. My newfound freedom was looking like it was going to be short-lived.

"Oh no, oh no, oh no." He put his hands over his ears to drown out the sound.

I put a reassuring hand on his shoulder and peered over the wall. Two of the building's doors popped open into the backs of the troops guarding them. Three female orderlies burst out the openings and over the fallen troops only to be tackled by the other soldiers. Groups of soldiers held each woman down. The soldiers picked the women up and carried them kicking and screaming back into the building. The women pleaded with the soldiers, pointing at the building and making biting and clawing gestures.

"Now's our chance."

I grabbed Alex by the collar and dragged him away from the building.

"What's going on?"

"People tried to escape. Just stay low."

We stayed low to the ground, struggling to move quickly without drawing the soldiers' attention. Trucks pulled up as we reached the side of the building. We stood and broke into a sprint. It was still early enough that there were few people out on the street. Still, we cut down an alley a few blocks from the building and didn't stop running until we were a good mile away. Alex put his hands on his knees and wheezed in and out with each breath.

"Here, here, put your hands behind your head. There you go, now look up at the sky—it'll help you breathe."

I propped Alex up behind a dumpster and looked up and down the alley. The alley was quiet and still and there were no signs of anyone pursuing us. Even though the reeking trash was overpowering, freedom smelled sweet.

12.

As we moved through damp alleyways and crisscrossed city blocks, I was surprised by the familiar surroundings interrupted occasionally by tall, undulating towers plated in translucent solar panels.

"Are we in Harlem?"

"Yes, we are," Alex answered while looking nervously behind us.

"I can still recognize the place. I used to come here a lot on business. Where are we going?"

"My apartment."

"You think it's safe?"

"Better than staying out on the street dressed like this. We need to get you in some normal clothes. Plus, it'll take them a while to piece together that we aren't in the building. I know some other places we can go later on."

"Where is your place?"

"Couple more blocks. It's over on a Hundred and Twenty-seventh."

The streets were bustling with late-morning traffic. As we waited to cross One Hundred and Twenty-fifth Street, I watched the morning commuters making their way to their destinations and began to feel as if I was in China. Everyone behind the wheel of a car was Asian.

Alex led me to the third floor of an ancient brownstone with cracked walls and a weathered, dilapidated front door. Alex's apartment was a reflection of himself. It was uncomplicated, carefully organized, and sparsely decorated.

I leaned against the back of a sagging maroon couch.
"How'd you know they were going to seal off the
building like that?"

"Oh. I've seen that happen a thousand times."

I gulped. I read too many comic books as a kid, and my
mind flooded with horrific images of futuristic societies
where all hell has broken loose.

"Really? A thousand times before? People attacking each
other and all that?"

"For heaven's sake, no. I've never seen *anything like that.*
I meant the quarantine. The government is always putting
up quarantines—buildings, city blocks, even entire cities at
times. A lot of the warfare these days is biological. You have
two sides that want each other's territory and, by and large,
they want it intact. Especially here. The Chinese
government has weaved their operations into the city. They
keep us Americans living here working for them, which
keeps the US military from destroying the city. I don't know
if they'd be willing to take out New York anyway, but at
some point I'd bet they would do it if it would help them to
get the country back. With a couple million civilians still
living here it takes wiping the city out off the table."

"So they'll kill us with germs instead?"

"Some of us, I suppose. They're constantly making
biological attacks against the Chinese military and
government institutions. Problem is, the Chinese are really
good at isolating the outbreak and treating the infected.
Their medicine is so advanced that the casualties tend to be
very low. Bombing has killed more civilians on this side
than bio warfare."

"That thing, you know, the," I hissed and made claws and
fangs at Alex, "that Barry, Elliott, and Janet got, was that
from a biological attack?"

"No, definitely not. The doctors isolated the origin virus. It was human polyomavirus, JCV."

"What is that?"

"We all have it, actually. Children get it from their parents. But something about the reanimation process caused the JCV to mutate radically in those three. Up until the last moment, the doctors thought they were dealing with a variola virus."

"A what?"

"You know, like smallpox. When they were trying to make sense of Elliott, they finally realized that it wasn't a variola after all. It was the JCV, but it had mutated so much that they hardly recognized it."

I didn't understand everything Alex was saying, but one thing was clear—just like the other cryonics, I had all the ingredients for the super virus. Thinking about coming down with their illness made me paranoid. I began to feel warm and clammy like I was coming down with a fever, but I chocked it up to hypochondriasis.

"So does that mean I have it?"

"I don't know. You didn't have the mutation in your preliminary exams, but neither did the others. It mutated so quickly. They were talking about testing you when all hell broke loose."

"What was up with that anyway? How come the doctors thought Elliott was dead when he wasn't?"

"He was dead."

"He *was*? He didn't look dead to me. I'd say he was pretty alive and hungry when he was having Dr. Feng for breakfast."

"I know, I know. That's what was so strange. In the beginning he was breathing, but his oxygen levels kept dropping as if he wasn't. His lungs weren't even obstructed, but he was way past the point of not getting enough oxygen to his brain. The alarm finally went off because his heart stopped, but his oxygen levels had reached zero long before that."

"All right, so he visited the other side for a little bit. He fired back up pretty nicely after that. Same thing happens to drowning victims."

"I wish that were it. I took a look at his vitals after he attacked that first doctor. He didn't have a pulse. He wasn't breathing, either."

"Muscle spasms?" I was joking, but part of me hoped Alex would agree.

"Did Janet and Barry look like they were having spasms? Or how about Elliott when he chased Dr. Feng down the hall?"

"Is that why you were being such a coward in there?"

"I don't know. I don't claim to be a particularly courageous person. The whole thing got under my skin."

"Well, if I start breaking out in sweats and sores you can just go ahead and take me out before I start biting."

"I'll keep my fingers crossed that it doesn't come to that," Alex said as he walked into the other room. He stepped back into the doorway and pelted me with something. "Here, put this on."

I held what Alex had thrown at me. It was a navy blue jumpsuit that buttoned in the front. I reluctantly removed my hospital clothes and slid on the jumpsuit. Alex returned from the bedroom wearing the same.

"Sweet, we're twins!" I exclaimed sarcastically.

"This is standard issue for civilians. We'll be a lot less noticeable on the streets in these."

"Well, we're ready to take out the trash."

"Come on, let's go. I know a place where they won't be looking for us."

13.

Alex led me back across town to a high-rise residential tower directly across the street from the facility we had escaped that morning. He assured me his friend Celeste's apartment was safe because she had told him they'd already searched the building for us, but we snuck in through a back entrance just to be safe.

When he knocked on a fourth-floor door, an absolute beauty answered. Celeste was tall and lithe with wavy jet-black hair and bright blue eyes that sparkled when she smiled. Her roommate Carson was another story. Alex had attempted to prepare me for him, but no description was adequate. Years before, Carson had been labeled a dissenter by the Chinese for trying to organize a labor strike. His attempt to get a day off for US citizens earned him a trip to a reeducation camp, where they lobotomized him and tinkered with his brain until he returned a model Chinese citizen. The three of them had been friends forever, and Celeste roomed with Carson so that she could keep an eye on him.

Carson was like an overzealous den mother offering us rice and asking all sorts of questions about where I'd come from and what my interests were. The four of us sat down for a bite and some tea, and I couldn't resist picking his brain.

"So what is it you do, Carson?"

"Royce, I'm so glad you asked. I'm a supervisor at the waste management facility."

"What sort of supervising do you do there?"

"I ensure the workers process the waste efficiently and accurately to support the great republic."

"Is that so? And processing trash is pretty important to the great republic, is it?"

"Oh yes. A clean society is an effective society."

"You sound like a pretty big fan of this great republic."

"I love the republic above all else."

"And why is that?"

"The great republic is creating peace and harmony throughout the world by integrating its cultures. The great republic provides for all the needs of its citizens. We have ample employment, shelter, and nourishment for our bodies. I am grateful to the great republic for everything it has given to me, and I dedicate my life to furthering its cause."

"Oh, that is just sick!"

"Royce, please," Alex begged.

Alex may have been uncomfortable with my toying with Carson, but Celeste was working very hard to suppress her laughter.

"I don't feel sick," Carson said. He was confused by the back and forth.

"No, I'm sure you don't, knucklehead."

"What's a knucklehead?"

"You're a knucklehead."

"Oh that's terrific. Thank you."

I left Carson alone after that for Alex's sake. If it wasn't for Alex helping me escape, I'd probably have been in a reeducation camp already. Though I still couldn't figure out why Alex had helped me in the first place. He definitely didn't seem the type to take it to the man, and our freedom was looking like it was going to be short lived. When we first came to Celeste and Carson's building, I'd actually wondered if Alex had brought us there to turn me in, but the longer we hung out, the more it seemed like that wasn't going to happen.

14.

The following morning after breakfast, Carson headed out to pick up their food rations for the week. I left Alex and Celeste at the table and stood at the window to watch the front of the building across the street. More soldiers had arrived and spread out in formation around the building. The street between our buildings was deserted as soldiers had blocked all vehicle traffic at both ends of the block. It was difficult to see in the few windows facing my direction, but there appeared to be a lot of movement happening behind them, maybe even some commotion.

Celeste rose from the table and joined me at the window. She placed both hands on the sill and gazed down at the street below.

"So where you from?" I asked.

"All over, but I was living here in the city when the war started. You?"

"California."

"So how did you end up out here?"

"Um, that's complicated. Didn't Alex tell you?"

"He said you're part of some kind of experiment they're doing in the lab."

"That all?"

"Wow, look at the ego on you. You'll be surprised to know that we weren't just sitting there talking about you."

Her comment stung a little, but it was hard to argue with her point. Since being reanimated, I had been pretty selfish. I was having a hard time accepting that this wasn't some kind of game, that these were real people I was dealing with.

"Ya, I guess I um . . . whoa! Look at that!"

I pointed toward the entrance to the building across the street. Several wild-eyed soldiers were shuffling down the steps toward the soldiers standing in formation. The shuffling soldiers shared a similar gait, each man limping and dragging himself along as if someone had broken one of his ankles. The soldiers surrounding the building maintained their formation, with their backs to their approaching colleagues. When the first soldier from the building reached the formation, he grabbed one of the men by the shoulders and bit deeply into the side of his neck. The trailing members of the party followed suit, biting and tackling men in the formation to the ground.

"Alex, Alex, get over here. You gotta see this!" I yelled.

Alex ran over. His jaw dropped wide open.

The attacking soldiers were decorated, and the rest of the formation had remained in their positions out of deference to authority. When one soldier couldn't take it anymore, he turned and knelt to help a fallen comrade. A higher-ranking member ran over and yelled at him to get back into formation, but was promptly attacked by one of the carnivorous officers from the building. As soon as he went down, the rest of the soldiers broke formation, shots were fired, and all hell broke loose.

We stood there silently absorbing the chaos descending upon the scene below. Medical personnel, workers in hazmat suits, and soldiers flooded out of the building. Some ran for their lives, while others stumbled out with that awkward, bloodthirsty stride that meant only one thing. That's when I noticed Carson, his arms full of groceries, strolling down the sidewalk toward our building like everything was hunky dory across the street.

"Oh no, look. It's Carson."

Alex and Celeste followed my finger and saw him. They looked worried. The attacks had spread to our side of the street and up and down the block.

"I'm going down there," I said.

I ran for the door and took the stairs down to the first floor. When I came out front, I couldn't find Carson in the melee. A panicked tenant covered in blood pushed past me into the building. I crouched behind a car. Infected soldiers and doctors paced the street in front of me. A doctor in bloody white scrubs ambled in my direction. An automatic weapon stuck out of his back like a dorsal fin. The bayonet was lodged in his spine. He raised his nose in the air, turned toward me, and growled. I stumbled backward awkwardly, and he started moving in my direction.

I crawled under the car. The doctor lay down and tried to come in after me. He snarled and screamed as he reached in after me, but the gun in his back pressed against the bumper and stopped him from crawling in any further. Seeing one of them up close was terrifying. His eyes were dull and vacant, and when he opened his mouth to growl, a putrid stench emerged from deep within his abdomen. The skin on his fingers was stripped down to the bone from clawing and scratching. Somehow he was moving and alive though his body had expired. Beyond the bayonet in his spine, he had massive bite wounds in his neck that left the severed arteries dangling like drooping flower stems. I thought about jamming my heel into his face, but I hesitated. Alive or dead, it didn't feel right to smash somebody's face in.

Safely out of the doctor's reach under the vehicle, I looked around for Carson. I spotted him near the entrance to his building. He was lying on his back with a doctor of his own on top of him. The doctor was biting and clawing at Carson who was flopping about like a fish. I pulled myself out from underneath the vehicle and ran over to help him. Carson's groceries were pinned between him and the assailant, and they appeared to be keeping him alive. I grabbed the doctor by the shoulders and ripped him off Carson. The doctor flew back onto the pavement, then quickly turned in my direction and bared his teeth. I recognized him immediately. Dr. Feng.

A burning hatred engulfed me. I'd never wanted to kill anyone, but after everything he'd done to me, seeing Dr. Feng attacking Carson made me want to end him. He may have been dead already. Who knew for certain? All that mattered was he was up and moving and hurting people and I was going to put a stop to it. I walked calmly over to the car I had been hiding under. The doctor impaled by the assault rifle was struggling to get to his feet. I put my foot on his back, grabbed the butt of the rifle, and pulled it out of him as I thrust him back onto the ground. I turned around and saw Dr. Feng was back on top of Carson, who now had his hands free and was struggling to hold Feng out of biting range. I walked up behind Feng and drove the bayonet into the back of his skull. The blade protruded between his eyes and stopped less than an inch from Carson's cheek. Blood and cerebrospinal fluid dripped out the wound onto Carson's face.

I hadn't anticipated the blade was going to come so close to Carson. I was overcome by emotion and acted without thinking. Feng's limp body lay draped across Carson. I pulled the blade out and pushed him off with my foot. Carson looked terrified and confused. His jumpsuit was covered in blood and grains of rice. People were being attacked all around us, and the screaming increased. I helped Carson to his feet and retrieved what I could of the damaged rations. I couldn't pick up much because I wasn't letting go of the gun. I put Carson's arm around my shoulder and walked him over to the building entrance. As we opened the front door, we caught the attention of an infected nurse and soldier. I pushed Carson inside, and he fell to the floor. I followed him in, dropped the groceries, and began searching for something to block the glass doors.

I spotted a janitor's closet in the lobby and pulled the door open. Two brooms leaned against some rusted shelving. I grabbed them and ran to the front door. I leaned my shoulder into the glass and wedged the brooms into the door handles as the infected pushed on the door from the other side. Their furor was drawing the attention of other infected who lumbered over and joined them against the glass. They moaned, growled, and pushed against the glass, stressing the strength of the broom's ability to keep them out. I pushed the lobby desk against the doors while bloody hands smeared the other side of the glass. I helped Carson back up. As we headed to the elevator bank, a confused tenant approached the building from the outside. She screamed as the violent horde pounced upon her. They tore into her abdomen and devoured her flesh while we stood there on the other side of the glass waiting for the elevator.

I felt terrible about blocking the doors. I just didn't know what else to do.

15.

"Oh my God! Oh my God!" Celeste cried. "Are you two all right?"

I lugged Carson into the apartment, then shut and locked the door behind us.

"I'm fine," I said, "but I don't know about him."

Alex and Celeste helped me get Carson into his room. We laid him on his bed and stripped off his blood-soaked clothing. He was covered in bite marks and deep scratches. Carson didn't say anything while we cleaned his wounds. Then he fell into a deep sleep, and we left him alone. The three of us went into the kitchen and salvaged what we could of the rations. There was rice, dried beef, and canned bok choy and cabbage.

"What happened down there?" Celeste asked.

"You couldn't see?"

"A little bit, but you were out of our line of sight most the time," Alex explained.

"It's gotten ugly down there. Whatever my cryonic friends from the hospital had is spreading like mad. Carson got attacked, and you're not going to believe who did it."

"Who?"

"Dr. Feng."

"What did he attack him with?"

"His teeth and nails."

"You mean he turned into one of those . . . one of those things?"

"Yes. When Elliott bit him, he must have passed the virus on to him. Pretty much all the doctors and nurses down there have it."

"This is not good," Alex muttered under his breath.

"That's not the worst of it. Remember when we were trying to figure out if the infected cryonics were alive or dead?"

"Of course."

"Well, they're definitely dead. I pulled that machine gun from the spine of one of Feng's henchmen. He was walking around like it wasn't even there, and his throat was ripped to shreds—arteries hanging out and everything. He was completely bled out."

"What are you two talking about?" Celeste asked. "Dead people don't just get up and walk."

"We had vitals hooked up to these people, and they were completely flatlined, walking around the room attacking people like wild animals," Alex explained.

"And they're trying to get into the building."

"They are?" Alex looked terrified. He ran over to the window and pressed his nose against the glass.

"It's OK. I mean, we should be OK. I blocked the front door pretty good."

We stood at the window. The crowd had thinned a bit, and bodies littered the street. Gunfire rattled from multiple directions.

"What's our next move, Al? Wait for the Chinese to come and clean up this mess?"

"Yes, they'll send in reinforcements and have this area quarantined by morning."

"I wouldn't be so sure of that," Celeste said.

16.

We went to sleep that night with a false sense of calm. The streets below us were quiet, and Carson slept soundly in his room.

A light moan from behind Carson's door snapped me out of my slumber on the living room couch. I'd heard that moan before. Like a student who realizes he forgot he had an exam, I was on my feet and freaking out that we'd failed to connect the dots.

I ran over to Celeste's room and yanked the door open, nearly hitting Alex, who was sleeping on the floor.

"Alex, Alex, wake up!" I yelled, shaking him. "It's Carson. He's got the disease."

"He doesn't have a disease," Alex said, pulling the covers over his head.

"Wake up, you idiot! He was bit by Dr. Feng. Dr. Feng bit him! That means he has the cryonic disease. We have to do something."

Alex pulled the covers down, and looked at me wide-eyed. He leapt up, and we stormed into Carson's room. He was covered in sweat, writhing and moaning in his sleep.

"What if it's just a fever?" Alex asked. "It might not mean anything."

"Alex, you didn't have to sleep in the same room as those freaks. I know what's going on here."

"What's wrong with Carson?" Celeste asked, stepping into the room. She wore a long silk nightgown that hugged her frame at her chest and hips. I tried not to look. Her figure made it hard to concentrate.

"Nothing . . . he'll be fine. It's just a fever," Alex said with a smile.

"Come on, guy! You know better than that. Celeste, he has the disease just like those people down on the street, and pretty soon we're going to have a homicidal maniac on our hands."

"What do we do?" she asked. "How can we stop it?"

"We can't," I explained, "unless we stop *him*."

"You mean kill him?"

"Nobody is going to kill your roommate," Alex said. "We don't know for sure that he has it. It's just a fever."

Carson groaned and looked around the room. Alex walked over to the bed.

"You all right, buddy?" Alex asked, stroking Carson's hair off his forehead.

Carson didn't respond. He looked right through Alex, then threw his head back against the bed, and stopped breathing. I ran over.

"Alex, he is *not* breathing," I said. "You know what's next."

"What's next?" Celeste asked.

"I'll tell you what's next." I ran out of the room and retrieved the machine gun. "We put an end to this before he hurts somebody."

"You can't just shoot him!" Alex shrieked.

I looked over at Celeste, who looked at me and shrugged. I put the gun down, ran into the living room again, and retrieved a wooden baseball bat from a wall display.

"Fine, I'll just hit him with this."

"No, not that," Celeste insisted. "Geronimo Pacheco hit a game-winning home run with that bat."

"Geronimo who?" I asked.

"Pacheco. You must not be a baseball fan."

"You won't find a bigger baseball fan," I huffed.

"He was after your time," Alex intervened.

"What do you mean *after* his time?" Celeste asked. "That homer couldn't have been more than fifteen years ago."

I looked at Alex incredulously. "You didn't tell her about me?"

"Tell me *what?*" Celeste asked.

Our ridiculous bickering had shifted our attention away from Carson who was now out of the bed and heading for Alex.

"Alex, look out!" I yelled.

Carson grabbed hold of Alex and went in for the bite, but Alex knew what to expect and held him back by the throat. Carson growled and shrieked. Alex's pencil-thin arms looked like they'd give way at any moment. I looked for the gun and was contemplating bullet or bayonet when Celeste jumped onto Carson's back and tried to pull him off Alex. The trio fell back onto the bed and rolled around wildly. I knew there was no way I could use the gun safely so I gripped the bat tightly and walked over to the bed. Carson was sandwiched between the two of them with Alex holding his arms from behind and Celeste pushing his face away from hers. I waited until they rolled onto their sides so that I could get a good look at Carson's head. As soon as they did, I swung the bat down with all my might. I felt his skull cave in beneath the pressure of the bat. His arms were still moving so I hit him a couple of more times for good measure. Each stroke of the bat splattered Alex and Celeste with blood.

I stood there, breathing heavily above Carson's lifeless body. Alex and Celeste lay motionless on either side of

Carson, their faces polka-dotted with blood. The room was dead silent. We stared at one another until the adrenaline subsided. That's when we heard it—a chorus of moans from the streets below the building. We ran over to the window. It was still dark out, and the building across the street, adjacent to the lab, was engulfed in flames. The blaze illuminated the swarm of undead roaming the streets below. There were hundreds, maybe thousands, of them moving in every direction. The disease was spreading.

17.

"We better go check the barricade on the front door. You two come down with me, and we'll make it stronger."

I grabbed the gun, Alex gave Celeste the bat, and we made our way out into the hallway. We heard thumping and screaming coming from one of the apartments at the other end of the hallway.

"You know your neighbors?" I asked Celeste.

"Yes, most of them, but I'm not sure which apartment that noise is coming from."

"Maybe we can check on them when we get back. We better go and take care of that door first."

"Let's stay out of the elevators," Alex said. "We don't want to get stuck in there."

"Good thinking, Al."

After we passed the third floor, the concrete stairs were smeared with fresh blood.

"Looks like your barricade didn't hold," Alex said.

"Could be. Or maybe somebody brought it in the building."

When we reached the lobby, we found the barricade still intact. We went into the janitor's closet and dragged the shelving out. We piled on toolboxes, paint cans, and anything we could find to add weight. The barrier left a lot to be desired, but we had very little to work with. A sea of infected made their way up and down the street on the other side of the glass. If something inside the building caught enough of their attention (or worse, someone opened the doors), everyone in the building was done for. With that in mind, we tiptoed back into the stairwell.

When we reached the second floor, I caught a glimpse of someone walking past the stairwell door. I stuck my face up to the tiny window to see what it was and was promptly greeted by a bloody, slobbering mess of bared teeth.

"Oh shit!" I screamed, jumping back in fear. "Looks like somebody brought it in the building."

"Either that or they got in through the parking garage," Alex said.

I aimed the rifle at the doorway and waited. Celeste joined me, bat in hand, and Alex stood in the corner looking nervously up and down the stairwell. The creature clawed and scratched at the thick steel door. It rammed the door violently with its head and shoulders, producing nothing more than a smear on the glass from the effort. It attacked the door so violently and screamed so loudly that we thought it would burst through at any moment. After a couple minutes of standing guard, we realized that we were safe behind the door.

"Apparently, they don't know how to turn doorknobs," I said with a chuckle.

"Lucky for us," Celeste added.

We grabbed Alex and ran up to Celeste's floor. The doorway at the end of the hall was open. Two of the infected were on the floor eating what was left of someone.

"Should we do something?" Alex asked.

Alex's comment captured the creatures' attention. As soon as they saw us, they started hustling in our direction.

"Fuck that, let's just get into the apartment," I said, opening the door and beckoning my companions inside.

We slammed the door shut. The ghouls in the hallway howled and scratched on the other side for several minutes but then abandoned us to return to their meal.

"I know them. They're my neighbors. That was their little boy they were eating."

"Oh, no. I'm sorry, Celeste," I said gently, resting my hand on her shoulder. "You two should go and get cleaned up. Take your mind off things for a minute. I'll stay out here and make sure we don't get any uninvited guests."

"I'll go in Carson's room," Alex said. "You don't need to see that."

Alex and Celeste headed back into the bedrooms. Things remained quiet on the other side of the apartment door so I put the gun down and went over to the windows to look outside. It was just past dawn, and what I could see of Harlem was in ruins. Smoke from building fires dotted the landscape. The streets were overrun with undead in every direction. It was clear the Chinese weren't going to be coming in to save us. We were trapped.

Alex and Celeste emerged from the bedrooms looking clean and composed. I pointed to the scene outside the apartment.

"I think we need to go."

"Go where?" Alex asked.

"Away from all this." I motioned at the street below. "Outside the city."

"We'll never make it."

"You need to realize something, Alex. It won't be long before all of them make their way in here, and that will be the end of us. Just look down there. You see that horseshoe-shaped crowd in front of the building? Those freaks are trying to get through our front door."

"Still, they can't open doorknobs, and we don't have a car. We can't just run for it," Alex said.

"Carson has a car," Celeste said with a smile. "They gave him one when they promoted him to supervisor."

"There we go, Al."

"We'll never make it out of the city. Americans are not allowed to leave the city without authorization. They have checkpoints."

"We'll never know until we try, but if we stay here, they'll eventually break that door down. That's certain."

"And there isn't much food here for three people," Celeste added, sorting through the rations.

"We're going to have to come out eventually. Isn't it better to do it now, before the building is overrun?"

"I don't know, I don't know," Alex fretted, pulling back his hair with both hands and pacing around the room. He stopped and looked out the window. I thought he was building nerve, but then he got that white-faced look—the same look he had when I needed him to free me from the hospital bed. "We should just wait it out. The army could come storming through here any minute, and then we'll be fine."

"Oh, really? We'd be fine, huh? What do you suppose the army is going to do with us when they find us? Two fugitives and a person harboring them? We'd be better off with the freaks."

I could tell Celeste was on board, but Alex sat down and put his head in his hands. He couldn't be convinced, but I wasn't going to leave without him.

18.

The moans and wailing inside the building grew louder as the day wore on. They were so piercing in the evening hours that we only mustered a few hours of terrified, restless sleep. By lunch the following day, it was clear the building was being overrun. People were jumping from the floors above us, and screams emanated through the floor.

I looked through the peephole. At least a dozen zombies paced up and down the hallway and scratched on doors.

"You think they busted through the barricade?" Celeste asked.

"I don't know, I just don't know." Our inactivity was making me nervous. I started pacing, racking my brain, and eyeballing Alex for any sign he'd changed his mind. "How many people live in this building?"

"A thousand. Maybe a couple thousand."

"Are a lot of them home this time of day? I mean, when all of this started happening?"

"No more than twenty-five percent."

Alex chimed in. "They keep us working in shifts so that people can't gather in large groups."

"Maybe that's all that's out there, people from the building. I don't see any soldiers or doctors. Here, take a look," I said to Celeste, giving her the peephole. "Are they your neighbors?"

"Most of them, yes."

"Then we still have a chance."

Celeste nodded. I could tell she was ready to make a move. Alex on the other hand was over by the window, staring blankly at the street below. I heard snorting and growling at my feet. I got down on my hands and knees and looked through the crack at the bottom of the door. I couldn't see much, but I could hear one of them sniffing at the crack. The growls turned to screams.

"Oh shit! It can smell us in here." I got up and looked through the peephole. The shrieking zombie was drawing the attention of the others down the hall. "I know how to stop this," I said with a smile. "Plug your ears."

I grabbed the assault rifle, released the safety, and got back on the floor. I pushed it against the crack and waited for the sniffing to come near. As soon as I heard sniffing near the barrel I pulled the trigger. The gun went off, and we heard a loud shriek followed by a light thump.

"I think I got him," I said excitedly, jumping up to look out the peephole. I saw a pair of feet, heels up at the bottom of the frame, but I didn't get to revel in my kill. The noise from the gun attracted the other zombies, who attacked the door ferociously. They pounded on the door and rammed into it until the hinges started coming loose.

"Oh, man, I did it now," I said sheepishly to my companions.

"They're going to break the door down. How many of them are out there?" Celeste asked calmly.

"About a dozen."

"How can they even do that? Do they have some kind of superhuman strength?"

"I don't think so. They just don't feel any pain. They'll keep ramming it until they break in."

"It's time to go," Celeste declared. "Alex, get the keys from the drawer in Carson's nightstand."

Alex didn't move. Celeste picked up the gun and walked over to him.

"We're out of time, dear. We have to go," she said sweetly. Alex stared at his shoes. She held the gun up by the muzzle, and her voice grew stern. "Come on, Alex. We can do this. This is a powerful weapon."

I grabbed the keys and ran around the apartment gathering food and clothing. I threw what I could in a duffle bag I found in Carson's closet. When I came back out into the living room, the front door was beginning to tilt into the apartment. Macabre fingers wriggled along the length of the gap. I went straight to Alex and handed him the bat.

"Alex, it's time," I said. He wouldn't even look at me. "This is just like when I was strapped on that bed across the street. If you stand there frozen, we die. If you move, we live." I put my hands on his shoulders. "You saved my life, buddy. I'm not going to let you die."

Alex held up the bat sheepishly, and we moved him toward the door. Celeste took charge. "Royce, I'm going to have you open the door, and then you two just follow me, but *stay behind me*. You do not want to get in front of this thing."

"You don't have to take the lead," I said. "I can do it."

"Actually, I do. Someone has to show you how to use this thing."

Celeste pointed the gun at the ceiling and pushed a button on the side. The bayonet retreated, and a thick, red laser beam emerged. It nearly reached the ceiling but cast no light upon it.

"Ok, just be sure to aim for the head. Shots to the body don't seem to kill them."

Celeste smiled at me wryly. I crouched down next to the doorknob and waited for her signal. When she was ready I yanked the door open so hard that I fell back on my ass.

Celeste stepped forward into the doorway like a gladiator and waved the laser back and forth at the zombies. The powerful beam seared through them like a hot knife through butter. They were in pieces on the carpet before I could get to my feet.

The hallway was littered with body parts and blood. Deep cuts and burn marks lined the walls where the laser had made contact. The jaws of severed heads chomped blindly like wind-up novelty teeth. A ghoul severed at the waist pulled itself slowly toward us.

"Holy shit, Celeste! That was incredible!" I squealed like a schoolgirl. She pushed the button on the side of the gun, and the metal bayonet returned from its sheath. "Did you know she was going to do that?"

Alex shook his head.

"Watch out for those heads, guys. They're still moving pretty good," I said.

As we tiptoed through the carnage, Celeste forced the bayonet into the skull of the crawling zombie. I heard a shucking sound behind me, like someone had tossed a pumpkin out the back of a moving pickup truck, and turned. Alex was smashing the active skulls with the baseball bat.

"Atta boy, Al. That's the spirit." I patted Alex on the back, and he smiled at us. It was the first time I'd seen him smile since the beginning of the outbreak.

We followed Celeste into the stairwell. Each time we reached a new floor, the zombies on the other side of the door shrieked and pounded against it as soon as they saw or smelled us.

When we reached the first floor, we paused before opening the door. The entrance to the parking garage was on the other side of the lobby, and the door in front of us was windowless. Celeste turned on the laser, and I took a deep breath before pulling the door open. To our delight, the barricade had held, and the lobby was clear. We strolled out into the open feeling victorious, but as soon as the ghouls out front saw us, they began pressing against the glass doors and climbing on top of each other en masse to get inside. The glass caved in under the pressure, and a sea of ghouls chased us in to the garage.

The zombies were so close behind us that we didn't even try to close the door. Celeste sliced and diced them as they erupted through the doorway. Alex handed me the bat, grabbed the key, and went off searching for Carson's vehicle.

I was standing behind Celeste with the baseball bat, impotently watching her work her magic when I heard Alex scream. I ran over to help and found him backed against a wall between two cars with a zombie closing in. It must have already been in the garage because none of them were getting past Celeste. I cracked the zombie in the back of the head with the bat, and it dropped to the ground.

Alex went looking for the vehicle while I searched the garage for more stragglers. Most came after me as soon as they saw me, and the bat was a formidable weapon against a single attacker. Occasionally, I wouldn't get a clean enough shot to the head, and they'd get back up after falling to the ground. One even took the blow like the bat was made of foam and got in close enough to get a hand on me. The thing with the ghouls is they were clumsy, so I was able to push him to the ground and finish him off with the bat.

"Found it!" Alex yelled from across the garage.

I sprinted over to him and saw that Carson's "truck" was actually a white delivery van with no back windows. I hopped in, and we motored to Celeste.

"Swing around in front of her so that we can get between her and the freaks. Just watch out for that laser."

Alex smashed into the zombies moving toward Celeste, and I opened my door. She hopped right on my lap, and we took off for the exit, ecstatic to be free from the menacing hands that thumped against the back of the van as we sped away.

19.

I expected the streets to be clogged with vehicles trying to flee, but so few civilians were allowed to drive that our biggest obstacle was the swarm of zombies wandering the roadway. Alex took pleasure in smashing into them, and he hit so many with such force that he had to turn on the windshield wipers to clear away the blood.

We drove straight up Broadway and hit the first checkpoint as we crossed the George Washington Bridge into New Jersey. We approached slowly. The checkpoint had been overrun. Infected soldiers ambled about along with a mix of the city's denizens. At the far end of the checkpoint, a heavily armed troop transporter stuck on a concrete barrier was surrounded by zombies. The driver was trapped in the cabin.

"Hey, wait. Stop a minute. You see that?" I asked, pointing toward the back of the carrier. The door was open, and the remains of the troops who had been devoured as they exited were scattered.

"Ya, I see him, but we don't want to help that guy," Alex said.

"No, not him," I explained. "Look at the back . . . on the ground. See all those guns? We should get those."

"It's not worth it," Celeste said. "What if something happens to one of us?"

"Yes, we can find more elsewhere," Alex chimed in.

"Just wait a minute, I have an idea. Celeste, give me the gun. How long can I make this thing?"

I rolled down my window and turned on the laser, pointing it laterally outside the vehicle.

"Um, it'll go about ten feet, I think. Just push this button to change the length."

I followed her instructions and extended the laser as far as it would go. "OK, Al, now drive me up alongside them."

Alex drove slowly toward the transporter. When the zombies saw us coming, some started moving in our direction.

"Step on it, Alex! We need to get them while they're all together."

Alex accelerated, and I leaned outside the window. I pushed my tongue between my lips slightly. I was concentrating so hard on finding the right height to do the most damage. We whizzed by the crowd, and the burning laser cut them in two at the head, neck, or shoulders. Alex circled around to survey the damage.

"Hot dog," I said, laughing. "Would you look at that? That worked like a charm. OK, buddy, loop me around again, and we'll get the rest of them near the back."

One more pass with the van, and we took the crowd out at the back of the troop transporter. I had Alex stop the car, and I hopped out to pick up the weapons. There were six assault rifles just like the one we already had and a big round silver grenade. I opened the back of the van, laid the rifles inside, and picked up the grenade before the zombies further away started coming. I hopped in the back, closed the doors, and we were on our way down the Turnpike.

I crawled to the front of the van and sat in the middle behind Alex and Celeste. I reached forward and squeezed Alex's shoulder. "Nice driving back there, buddy. We made a pretty nice haul. What do you suppose this weird-looking grenade is?" I held it out between them so they could have a look.

"Careful with that one. That's a neutron grenade," Celeste said.

"You mean it's nuclear?"

"Yessirree. Creates a controlled nuclear explosion within a fifteen-foot radius."

I put the grenade in a compartment at the back of the van. It didn't seem wise to be carrying a nuclear device in my pocket. I inspected the guns we retrieved to make sure they were in working condition. "These things are incredible. Hey, Celeste, where'd you learn how to use guns like that?"

"I was an army brat. My dad always took my brother and me shooting. He made sure we knew how to use the latest and greatest. Always said we'd never know when we might need to use one."

"Guess he was right about that. Say, where's your family now?"

"My parents were living in Boca Raton when the waves hit."

"Did they make it out OK?"

"I don't know. The last time I spoke to them was a few days before it happened."

"The tsunami crippled all communication in the East, and then the Chinese reestablished it for their own purposes. We don't have access," Alex explained.

"You said you're from the West, didn't you?" Celeste asked.

"Um, yes."

"They don't explain what's going on out here to you?"

"Well, you see, I'm different. I um—"

"Oh, I get it. He's one of those failed lobotomies, isn't he?" she asked Alex.

"No, Royce is different."

"How so?"

"He's a cryonic."

"What's a cryonic?"

"He was cryogenically frozen in twenty ten."

"When I died," I added with a wink.

"You can't be serious. I thought that was next-century technology?"

"Not for the Chinese," Alex said. "Though Royce is the only one. There were three others, but they're, well, they were the source of the outbreak."

"Why didn't you get sick?"

I shrugged. "I dunno."

Celeste sat quietly for a moment looking through the window. "So what year were you born?" she asked.

"Nineteen sixty-three."

"You must think the world is a really messed up place."

"It's pretty bleak."

"But look at you. You're alive again, and you're not like *them*. Not to mention you're free. Not too many people in this part of the country can say that."

She had a point. At least I liked her positivity, and her beauty made her message that much more convincing.

"So what about you, Alex?" I asked. "Where's your family?"

Alex's eyes welled with tears. "They were in Denver," he choked.

Celeste put a comforting hand on his shoulder. I didn't dare ask what had happened in Denver.

"A few years back," Alex said, composing himself, "the government decided to nuke Shanghai. The situation here wasn't changing, and they figured the Chinese wouldn't retaliate against territory they wanted to possess. They were wrong. The bombing of Shanghai was successful, and the Chinese retaliated immediately by wiping out Denver. It's been a complete stalemate ever since."

We sat for a time in silence. I wondered why the Chinese chose Denver. I figured they wanted to send a message without deleting territory that would jeopardize their future plans. Erasing Los Angeles or San Francisco would probably have destroyed valuable shipping ports on the West Coast.

I eyed Celeste's blood-stained baseball bat, which danced about on the floor of the van every time we hit a bump. I spoke to Celeste and tried to lighten the mood. "So you're a big baseball fan, huh?"

"Big time."

"What's your team?"

"Braves."

"Ninety-eight was nice. We *crushed* you in the NLCS. I went to every game."

"Ah, so I take it you're a Padres fan?"

"Guilty as charged."

"Well, I wasn't even born in ninety-eight."

"That's funny. I didn't even think about that. Say, did the Padres ever win a World Series? Cause you know they hadn't yet when I . . . well they hadn't yet in twenty ten."

"They most certainly did. Had a dynasty in the late twenties and early thirties. I think they won three times."

"Really? That's awesome."

"Nope. Just messing with you."

Celeste's joke made Alex laugh, and that made me smile.

20.

We left the 95 before we got to Baltimore and parked in a wooded area along the Chesapeake. It was summertime, and the evening air was thick and warm. It felt great to get out of the car and smell the trees. The shrill songs of cicadas resonated throughout the forest.

We were headed in one direction and that was to safety. Philadelphia and Wilmington weren't burning like Manhattan, but something wasn't right. The military checkpoints outside both cities were abandoned. Staying away from the infected and the Chinese was a tenuous proposition, and the woods felt like a safe bet.

We lit a fire with a laser near the back of the van and sat on logs. Alex cooked rice in a metal hard hat he had found in the back of the van. We hadn't eaten all day, and we devoured our meal in silence.

"Oh, man, I never thought rice could taste so good," I said.

"It's amazing how much better food tastes when you're starving," Celeste added. "We've had a lot of that over the last ten years."

"Where do you two think we should go?" I asked.

"I suppose there are places we could hide," Alex suggested. "The Chinese rounded everyone up and moved them into the cities after the war began, but there's rumors of independent settlements in the hills."

"You believe those stories?" Celeste asked.

"I don't know," Alex said. "I don't know what to believe."

"What about the West? You think we could make our way to freedom?" I asked.

"Fat chance," Celeste said.

"The front is heavily fortified, from the Gulf of Mexico to Canada. There are five million troops on the Chinese side alone," Alex explained.

"We'd never get past them. Besides, this feels an awful lot like freedom to me," Celeste said, stretching her legs out and laying her head against a log.

"We shouldn't sleep out here," Alex said nervously. "Just in case, you know, *they* come."

"Good idea, Al. It'll be a little tight, but it won't be the first time you two have spooned. Am I right?"

"You're hilarious," Alex said sarcastically.

"Ooh, Al . . . sarcasm. Let me hear some more of that. It suits you," I said with a grin.

We spread the extra clothes out in the back of the van, locked the doors, and called it a night. Although I was tired, I lay there thinking while Alex and Celeste slept. My family, whatever was left of them, was out West. I just knew it. They would never leave their hometown. The thought of living the rest of my life without seeing them again made me sick. I couldn't tolerate it. I wouldn't tolerate it. We were going to make it past the front, whether Alex and Celeste thought it was possible or not.

21.

The next few days in the woods were delightful. We were carefree, killing fish in the bay with the laser and shooting squirrels and rabbits with the guns. Killing fish with the laser made a mess of our catch, but it was ridiculously easy. We just turned it on and swiped the laser up and down across the water until something floated up to the surface. I found the hunting particularly fun. I even shot a couple of nutria that emerged from their burrows along the shoreline. They tasted like rabbits.

We got to know each other well, and our friendship blossomed. Turned out Alex and Celeste met before the war and had been friends ever since. Alex had a bug collection in college, and Celeste played baseball with the boys until she was in high school. I told them about my surfing habit, the thought of which got me obsessing about all of the empty waves peeling off unridden because of the war.

One evening, we were sitting around the campfire cooking the last of our rice. I started thinking about our next move.

"Where do you guys think we should go?" I asked.

"I've been thinking south," Celeste said. "It isn't going to stay warm forever, and we could work our way toward a better climate."

"What about food?" Alex asked. "There's plenty if we stay here."

"It's not like this is the only place to shoot a squirrel, Al. I'm more worried about that van. It's electric, right? Don't we need to plug it in or something?"

"It's solar," Celeste said.

"Wow, that's so cool. Where are the panels?" I asked.

"Panels?" Celeste asked, laughing. "You mean those big plastic things they used to put on top of homes?"

Even Alex chuckled. I shrugged.

"I'm sorry, Royce. It's in the paint. The whole van absorbs the energy from the sun. Not too many vehicles run on electricity or gasoline anymore," Celeste explained.

"What about when it's cloudy?"

"Doesn't matter. As long as you don't park it in the garage for a week or more it'll keep on running."

"Well, that's a bonus. We're going to make great time."

"That's assuming we have somewhere to go," Alex said. "The Chinese have a pretty tight grip on things, and once they see us—"

Crack! Someone or something stepped on a stick.

We grabbed our rifles and headed in the direction of the noise.

"Should I turn my laser on?" I whispered.

"Too dangerous," Celeste said. "Better to know you have a target before you start waving that thing around."

"Hello, is somebody there?" a voice called out from the woods. "I'm a friend. I'm . . . I'm unarmed."

"Show yourself," I barked.

A portly, pale man with a protruding belly and bright red hair stepped out from behind some bushes. He was sopping wet and wearing dirty white underwear.

"Who are you?" Celeste asked.

"I'm Mike. Mike Dexter. I just escaped from the Chinese."

"I'm Royce," I said. "This is Alex and Celeste. Come with us. We've got a fire. You can warm up."

Mike was thrilled to come back to our camp and get in a dry jumpsuit.

"Boy, I sure am glad I came across you three," he said. "How'd you end up out here?"

We told him about the outbreak and our journey from New York. Then we started asking questions.

"Why were you wet?" Alex asked awkwardly.

"I was on a boat. There was an outbreak on board. A field officer arrived with a secret message, then asked to be relieved of duty so he could rest. Next thing you know, he's running around attacking people. Before long, the whole ship was crawling with those things. I had to exit stage left."

"You were working for the Chinese?" I asked.

"They had me working as a secretary in a communication center for the military. I was an attorney before the war, and those bastards had me making coffee and taking out the trash. This is my first time off that boat in more than nine years. They disguise it as a cargo vessel to eliminate suspicion. Afraid our boys back west will pick up on it and take it out."

"How about the virus?" Alex asked. "Have they been able to stop it?" Mike looked at Alex like he was nuts. "I mean, elsewhere."

"Quite the opposite, actually. They think it is some sort of bioterrorism from the US side. Once they lost communication with the research center in New York, they started ferrying infected soldiers around the territory to their best research centers. They wanted to get to the bottom of this thing immediately so that they could stop it before the Americans fully implemented the campaign. They'd fly infected soldiers into a city, there'd be an outbreak, and they'd lose contact. They figured they were too late."

"But they're the ones causing it, not the Americans," Alex said.

"Makes sense to me now," Mike said. "Not so easy when you don't know what you know. It's complete chaos out there."

"Oh shit," Celeste said with a sigh. "They're spreading this thing everywhere."

"Where are the research centers where they sent the infected soldiers?" I asked.

"Let's see . . . there's Richmond, Macon, Cleveland, Sheboygan, Weston, Birmingham, Tallahassee, Charlotte, Charlottesville, Philly, DC, um, Bangor—"

"Ok, ok, we get the picture," I said. I glanced at Alex and Celeste. They looked as deflated as I felt. If there was a bright side to all of this, we weren't seeing it.

Mike continued. "They said solving this thing was job one so they wanted all of their scientists working with the infected. They even sent the sick home to their research centers in China."

"There goes Asia," I said.

"How'd you even pick up on all this?" Alex challenged. "Where I work, they only speak Chinese."

"Obviously, I speak Chinese. Unbeknownst to them, of course. Back before the war, there were a lot of Chinese businesses trying to make hay over here. They were snatching up property, buying US companies—the whole nine yards. I learned some of the language, and I cleaned up because I spoke it. Kind of poorly back then, but listening to their conversations for the last decade has sharpened my saw, so to speak. It's funny—eavesdropping on them was the only thing that kept me sane. I felt like a covert operative, even though I couldn't really do anything with the information."

"Why you giving him a hard time, Al? You learned Chinese working in the lab. What, you think you're smarter than everybody?"

"No, I just—"

"Well, Mike, you've stumbled upon the right group. We have guns, a car, and we had food, but I'm sure we can find some more. You can sleep with us in the van tonight, if you'd like, but you'll have to lie in the front seat. Things are pretty full in the back."

"Thanks you three, really," Mike said. "I mean it—I really appreciate it. I won't be a bother, I promise."

22.

It rained hard that night—so hard that we couldn't hear the slippery little fingers dragging along the outside of the van. The rain stopped well before dawn, and we awoke to the familiar sound of moaning.

"What's that? Who's there?" Mike asked while shifting about nervously in the front seat.

I recognized the sound and climbed immediately into the driver's seat to have a look. The windows were completely fogged up, and I couldn't see a thing.

"Hey, Alex, where's the defrost on this thing?" I yelled to the back.

Alex turned on the defrost, and we sat and listened to the moaning and scraping while we waited for the windows to clear.

"I wonder if it's the infected from the ship?" Mike asked. "You think they can swim?"

"We better pray it's them, and the outbreak didn't make it this far already. Otherwise, who knows how many are out there."

The windows cleared, but it was too dark outside to see our visitors clearly.

"All right, Al, now how about the headlights?"

Alex reached around the steering column and turned the headlights on. A zombie child wearing red shorts and a matching red-collared shirt with a bright yellow neckerchief wandered in front. Every few moments, another child circled in front of the headlights. They were all wearing the same thing.

"What are they, Cub Scouts?" I asked.

"Not exactly," Alex explained. "They're Imperial Apprentices. The Chinese make all kids go through it. You can imagine what they learn."

"Man, I really don't want to laser a bunch of kids. What do you say we move on?" Everyone was quick to agree. I put the van into gear and lurched forward, hitting the brakes as one of the boys stepped in front of the van.

"Don't run him over!" Alex squawked.

"Ok, ok, relax. It's not like a broken leg is going to keep him from earning a merit badge." I hated being told what to do, but Alex had a point. So, I waited until the path in front of the van was clear, and I stomped on the gas. The tires spun wildly in place, and I pulled my foot off the gas but it was too late; I could feel the back of the van sinking lower into the mud as the tires decelerated. I tried going backward, but it was no use. We were stuck.

"Well, fuck!" I yelled.

"Try rocking her back and forth," Mike suggested.

I looked at him incredulously. I'd been stuck in the mud and sand plenty of times on trips to Baja, and I knew there was only one way out of our predicament.

"Look, guys, I'm going to have to waste those kids."

"No, you can't," Celeste said, "there's got to be another way."

"But I have to get something under our tires. They know we're in here and I doubt their appetite is going to change anytime soon."

"Let's just wait it out," Mike said. "I'm sure they'll go away."

We sat in silence. When dawn came, the zombies could see us inside the vehicle and that just riled them up more.

Still, the top of the head of the tallest one barely cleared the bottom of the side window, so they couldn't break into our sanctuary. We crawled into the back of the van, hoping that if they couldn't see us they might calm down. It didn't work.

"Where do you think their scout master is?" I asked, hoping to kill the time. "Did anyone see him?"

"I didn't see him," Mike said. "You think they ate him?"

"Probably off in the bushes somewhere, or perhaps back at their campsite," Alex added.

By late morning, our stomachs were growling, and nobody had cracked, so I decided to be the bad guy. "Look, guys, they clearly aren't going anywhere. It's stupid for us to sit here just because we don't want to kill some infected kids. They're already dead so they're going to outlast us. We, on the other hand, are going to be dead if we don't get something to eat."

No one responded. I took their silence for complicity and grabbed a gun. I climbed into the passenger seat and said, "I'll just kill the ones I have to," before unlatching the door and kicking it open with my foot.

The three scouts against the door flew back on the ground. Any tinge of guilt I had evaporated as soon as I saw their dead eyes and slobbering gray scowls. I turned on the laser and sliced off their legs so they couldn't get back up to go after me. I turned and gave the thumbs up to the group watching from the window. Four more scouts stood near the back of the van. There were no windows there to expose my sins. I ran the laser right through their heads.

I stopped for a moment to survey the damage. The mud behind our rear tires was thick and deep. I was going to need something substantial to wedge in there and get us out. That's when I heard growling behind me. I turned around.

Another small zombie was running toward me. Much of his abdomen had been devoured, and his intestines hung loose and bounced around like sausages. At first I thought he was one of the children because he was small and wearing the same uniform, but as he came closer and I got a good look at his face I realized he was a tiny man—a little person.

I stood there in awe as he approached me, and after I ran the laser through the front of his head, I realized something—he was the perfect size to wedge behind our tire and get us out of the mud. I unleashed the bayonet and used it to clear some mud from behind the tire. Then I picked up the scout leader and stuffed him in the gap. I did the same with one of the kids on the other side of the van. I moved quickly to avoid the three crawling torsos still coming after me.

I knocked on the driver's side window, and they let me in. I climbed into the seat and placed my hands gently onto the steering wheel.

"How'd it go?" Mike asked from the passenger seat.

"Oh, it went all right."

"Did you find something to stick underneath the tires?" Celeste asked.

Now I was blushing. "Yes, yes, I did. Found their scout leader, too."

"Was he eaten?"

"They'd snacked on him a bit, but he was up and about."

"Really," Mike pondered, "I wonder why we didn't see him?"

"We did, we just didn't know it."

"What do you mean?" Alex asked.

"He was with the troop . . . right outside the van. We just didn't notice because he was a little person."

"A what?"

"You know, he was a . . . a *little* person. That's what we called them anyway. That or, well, there's another term, but it's kind of derogatory. Is that what you use?"

"Use what?" Celeste asked, exasperated.

"Midget?"

"Oh, now I know what you mean. No, no, no, the preferred term is growth limited," she explained.

"I like that better. Sounds sort of like a mutual fund. Seriously though, I always thought *little people* was kind of mean. Like they were somehow inferior to regular-sized people. Anyhoo, should we give it a try?"

"Yes, please. I'm hungry," Mike said.

I put the van into reverse and backed up over the bodies onto firm ground. We were on our way.

23.

We headed back on the highway and traveled south along the outskirts of Baltimore, which had clearly been overrun. Buildings smoldered. The dead lumbered along the 95 in packs. I made a game of plowing through packs of them with the van, until everyone told me to stop so that I wouldn't crash.

We drove to Silver Spring. Mike said there was a storage depot for rations. We figured it was better to stock up if we could, since we didn't know how long we'd be able to stay in the woods without being overrun. The van would keep us moving if we could just find somewhere to go. As long as we had food and water, it seemed like the way to go.

The storage depot was a massive warehouse located at the rear of a business park near the city center. The parking lot surrounding the building was absolutely inundated with ghouls. Soldiers, civilians, and office workers roamed every inch of the grounds. We stopped and watched them from a safe distance.

"How do you suppose we get in?" I asked Mike.

"Well, the delivery doors are closed. That's good and bad. Good because it keeps them out, but bad because a retina scanner is the only way inside the building."

I scrutinized the building and its surroundings and thought for a moment. "I have an idea. I can get us in the personnel entrance right there."

"You won't be able to cut through that door with the laser," Celeste said. "It's designed to cut through flesh. It won't go through metal that thick."

"That's all right. I have something else in mind." I crawled into the back of the van and pulled the neutron grenade from the compartment I'd placed it in. I put the grenade in my pocket and zipped it shut. "Celeste and Mike, grab a gun. We're going to have to fight our way in there." They looked reluctant to follow my suggestion. "Look, you might as well get used to this. As long as this thing keeps spreading, fighting these freaks is the only way we're going to stay alive. I know there's a lot of them out there, but we have frickin' laser beams for Chrissake."

Mike and Celeste each grabbed a weapon. Alex just sat there. "Don't worry, Al. You can drive on this one. We're going to need you to get the van inside the building as soon as we can open that delivery door. You see those three doors? Not those. They're for semis so they're elevated. That fourth door over there, on the left, that's you. After you drop us off, just keep moving so they don't break your windows, and as soon as you see the door open, gun it so we don't let too many of them inside. Got it?" Alex nodded. "Okay, now drive us up near the personnel entrance. Celeste, stick your laser out the window, and I'll sneak up here behind Alex and stick mine out his window. Alex, you drive in circles near the doorway until we clear a space for us to get out safely."

My plan worked beautifully. We cleared a large circle in the crowd and hopped out of the van. The zombies were quick to close the gap.

"Hey guys, cover me while I go and work on the door," I said, running toward the doorway. While Mike and Celeste sliced into the approaching herd, I searched the crowd for what I was after. I saw a portion of him lying there on the pavement, a uniformed officer cut horizontally across the chest by the laser. His arms were useless nubs, so he was using his teeth to pull himself inch by inch along the ground toward Celeste. I ran up behind her, picked him up off the ground, carried him over to the door, and held him up in front of the retinal scanner.

An automated voice spoke in Chinese. The door slid open.

"Guys, come on!" I yelled to Mike and Celeste, who turned off their lasers and made a beeline for the door. Once inside, Mike quickly found the button that sealed the door shut, and the three of us stood there panting, relieved to be safe inside. The warehouse was stocked floor to ceiling with food all loaded neatly onto pallets. One section was boxes of canned fruit and vegetables, another fifty-pound bags of rice, and the other cases of meats sealed in odd metallic bags.

Infected workers roamed the warehouse's towering aisles. We decided to split up and go looking for them. I went down an aisle loaded with rice on both sides. Two zombies at the other end charged. I decided I needed some practice shooting the gun so I fired at them as they charged me until I put bullets in their heads.

As I was about to turn the corner to the next aisle, a laser sliced through the bags stacked next to me and sent a cascade of rice spilling to the ground.

"Whoa, hey! Careful with that thing!" I yelled. I found Mike on the other side. He'd just disposed of an enemy and was fiddling with his gun, struggling to turn the laser off.

"Sorry about that. I'm still getting used to these things. I think that was the last one," Mike said.

"Celeste!" I yelled. "We all clear?"

"All clear over here," she answered.

"You're gonna like this stuff," Mike said, showing me a bag of meat that had fallen from a box. "You pull this cord right here, the chemicals kick off, and bam! It's like you just pulled it out of the oven on Thanksgiving."

24.

Celeste and I went to open the freight door while Mike had a look around. I rolled up my sleeves and pulled hard on the chain to crank the door open. As soon as the zombies wandering around outside saw us, they growled and shrieked and moved in our direction. Alex was right where he was supposed to be. He drove the van through the opening, knocking down some of the intruders in the process. I pulled hard on the chain to shut the door while Celeste took the laser to those who made it inside. A blood-curdling scream reverberated from the other end of the warehouse.

I dashed across the warehouse. Mike was near the wide-open doorway for the personnel entrance. Multiple ghouls were climbing on top of him as several more poured in. I sliced at the ghouls on top of Mike, and then focused on the doorway. The laser made quick work of those coming in, but a wall of bodies followed right behind. I charged into the doorway, hoping to clear enough room to get back inside and push the button to shut them out. That's when my gun beeped. The laser retracted, and the bayonet thrust forward in its place. I was stuck in hand-to-hand combat with attackers coming at me from more directions than my weapon could handle. I pulled the trigger and sprayed bullets, but the only ones who fell were those who took bullets to the head. Hands grabbed me on all sides, and then a mouth clamped down on my right forearm. The shock of the bite pulled my hand from the trigger, and a zombie in front of me became impaled on the blade, pulling the gun from my hands.

I could feel the heat from Celeste's laser as she decapitated my attackers from behind. Alex grabbed me by the collar and pulled me back inside, then waited patiently for Celeste to work her way back in. I looked over at Mike, who was screaming. He was bleeding profusely. I pulled my sleeve back to reveal the bite on my right arm. It looked like I'd been attacked by a dog. The bite was only a couple of inches across, but it covered the width of my forearm. I could make out the path of the top and bottom rows of teeth. The skin was broken all the way around. The bite wasn't deep, and the muscle remained intact.

I ran over to Mike, who was going into shock. Alex and Celeste were still distracted by the chaos in the doorway. I pulled some fabric from Mike's sleeve, tied it around my wound to stop the bleeding, and pulled my sleeve back down to hide it.

25.

Mike had chunks of flesh missing in several places. Both his thighs had hunks missing, but his right triceps was the worst. It looked like more than half of it was gone. I pulled more fabric from Mike's clothing and tied a tourniquet around his right armpit to cut off the flow of blood to his arm. Having successfully sealed the doorway, Alex and Celeste joined us. Mike's leg wounds looked less threatening, so we stuffed them with golf-ball-sized wads of fabric and tied fabric around the wounds to keep the wads in place.

Mike started coming to, and as always, he wanted to talk. "Thanks, guys, thanks. I don't know what happened. I was digging through that shelf near the doorway, and those fuckers got the door open somehow. Oh man, oh man, I'm in bad—"

The automated voice spoke and the door slid open.

"Close it for me, Al."

In one fell swoop, I grabbed Celeste's weapon and kicked the leading intruder back into the others and out the door. I unloaded rounds into them as Alex shut the door.

"It's that God-forsaken retina scanner. Those creeps are beating on the door looking for us, and every time a soldier is in front it opens the door for them."

"Guys, guys, just leave me here," Mike begged. "You gotta go. You know what's going to happen to me."

"No, we don't," I barked. "We're gonna load that van up with food, and then we're gonna . . ." I looked around the room as I searched desperately for an answer, "we're gonna take you to one of those research centers to see if they've found a cure."

The personnel door opened again. Celeste and Alex took care of it.

"Royce, we're not going anywhere if we can't do something about that door," Celeste said.

"I know, I know. Gimme a second. I gotta get another gun from the van. The laser on that other one crapped out on me."

"The gun is fine," she said. "You just used up the battery. Too much fishing."

"How do we charge those things?"

"With a charger, of course."

"Can we get one?"

"Not likely, unless we can get inside their barracks."

"I know what to do about the door. We can take that forklift and block it with pallets," Alex suggested.

"That might hold for a while, but there's too many of them," I said. "Remember, they don't feel anything so they'll just mash themselves into it until it falls over. We need more time than that to load the van. We won't be able to finish."

We stood there for a moment.

"I have an idea," I said. "Celeste, Alex, watch the door. Just, um, don't stand too close to it, okay? Unless they open it, of course."

They looked at me like I was crazy, which I guess I was. A ladder on the wall behind us led to the roof. I climbed the ladder and walked over to the edge of the roof directly above the personnel entrance. The zombies below massed around the entrance, pushing and pawing at it because they knew what was inside.

I pulled the neutron grenade from my pocket.

The zombies moved back and forth across the spot where I wanted the grenade to land. I needed a bit of a clearing to throw it into, otherwise it might bounce off somebody and land too close to the door. I couldn't help but notice that my predicament was a bit like playing a game at the county fair, except my friends would die if I messed up.

I waited and waited until the moment was right. Then I pulled the pin and tossed the grenade underhand toward the clearing like I was throwing a bocce ball. I was so concerned about the grenade landing too close to the door that I threw it too hard in the other direction. I watched the grenade's high arcing trajectory with bated breath. It cleared the area I wanted it to land in and plucked a zombie in the forehead who stepped into its path. The grenade careened off the ghoul's forehead and then hopped across the concrete before rolling to a stop in the middle of the clearing I was shooting for. I couldn't have put it in a better spot if I had walked it out there myself.

I was so busy reveling in my good fortune that I didn't think to hit the deck. When the grenade went off, the force of the blast took care of that for me. I flew backwards and landed flat on my back. I lay there for a moment watching the glory of a mini mushroom cloud. When the smoke cleared, I leapt to my feet and ran to the edge of the roof to check out the grenade's handiwork. Just as Celeste had promised, the crater from the blast was roughly fifteen feet in diameter. It was much deeper than I had expected, which was all the better. The zombies outside the blast radius fell into the crater one after another on their way to the door. Once in the crater they were too far away from the retina scanner for it to pick them up. The crater was just close enough to the door that zombies walking in from the sides couldn't get in front of the scanner without falling into the hole.

"What did you do?" Alex yelled to me as I made my way back down the ladder. "My ears won't stop ringing."

"It was the neutron grenade."

"Why bother?" Celeste asked. "There's no way you got all of them."

"Nope. Didn't get them all, but I did make a big ole hole in front of the door. They're all falling in, and now they can't get in front of the scanner."

"That's very clever, Royce," Celeste said with a warm smile.

"Happy to be of service. I'm probably going to get cancer from it, but . . . "

"Don't worry about cancer," Alex said. "It's not even a serious illness anymore."

"We better get some more of those grenades then," I said, grinning. "Seriously though, let's load the van before too many of those freaks fall in that hole, and they start piling on top of each other."

26.

Alex, Celeste, and I loaded the van as carefully as we could, trying to maximize the space available. We packed one side with boxes of meat and cans, and created a flat space with bags of rice on the other to lay Mike on.

Alex and I helped Mike up on his makeshift bed.

"Mike, we're going to take you to one of those research hospitals you told us about and get you fixed up," I said. Alex and Celeste wouldn't look at me or Mike. It was clear they didn't like my plan, but were uncomfortable speaking against it given Mike's predicament.

"I don't think that's a good idea," Mike said, groaning in pain. "It's a military hospital. They aren't just going to let the three of you waltz in and out of there as you please, and that's assuming they haven't been overrun."

"Let us figure that out. Your job is to hang on until we get you there, okay? Where'd you say the nearest facility was, DC?"

"Yes, DC."

"We shouldn't go to DC," Alex said. "It's too populated. We need a place that will have less of those things walking around."

"We can't go far. This guy doesn't have much time."

"That's true, but if we go to the capitol, we might not even make it, and where does that leave him?" Celeste had a point.

"Mike, is there another place we can go?" I asked. "Somewhere outside the city?"

Mike lay there looking at the ceiling. I couldn't tell if he was thinking or losing consciousness.

"We can go to Weston." He coughed. "It's a small town. There's a secret facility operating inside an abandoned insane asylum. It's about . . . eighty miles northeast of Charleston. Shouldn't take more than a few hours."

"Alex, Celeste, what do you think?"

"We can try," Celeste said.

"All right, I'll get the door."

They climbed in the van, and I walked over to the door and started pulling on the chain to open it. Each tug made my wound itch and burn. Once I got the door open, I climbed into the passenger seat next to Celeste, who was sitting between the seats on a sack of rice. I put my arm on the armrest to steady myself as Alex weaved through the zombies still wandering the business park. That's when I noticed the blood from my wound seeping through my sleeve. Celeste was looking out my window, and I pulled my arm down nervously between the seat and the door to hide the wound. I couldn't tell if she noticed, and I stared blankly out the window, unwilling to find out.

27.

By the time we reached Weston, Mike was passed out in the back of the van and dripping with sweat.

"You think he'll turn soon?" Celeste asked, checking on his condition.

"I hope not, but we better keep the guns handy just in case," I said.

It was dusk as we crawled down Main Street in the van. Weston was tiny. It reminded me of a movie set for small town USA that had long been abandoned. Tall weeds sprouted right through the pavement, and the cars parked along the curb were caked with dust. Other than the weeds and grime, some of the shops almost looked as if they were still taking business. We passed a restaurant that still had an open sign hanging in the window, and the filthy steel tables were still arranged neatly on the outdoor patio. Other shops were boarded up and riddled with bullet holes.

"What happened to this place?" I asked.

Alex didn't say a word, and Celeste was slow to answer. It was clear they hadn't been out of the city enough to see something like this. "After the invasion, the Chinese came into small towns and rounded everyone up. They wanted everyone in the cities so they were easier to control and put to work," she said.

"Looks like there wasn't much time to prepare."

"Most people didn't know it was coming. The Chinese took people from where they stood, rounded them up like animals, and hauled them off in caravans. Those who holed up and put up a fight were sent to the reeducation camps."

"So they left everything behind?"

"Everything."

"We should take a look around on our way out. You know, see what we can find."

"We should," Celeste said with a sigh.

28.

A brief detour off Main Street led us to the expansive grounds of the Trans-Allegheny Lunatic Asylum. The building itself was an ancient, rectangular stone structure with multiple floors and narrow wings stretching off into the distance. The stained, white clock tower at the center of the building seemed out of place against the portent Gothic architecture. The tower's peak was adorned with a large copper steeple that thrust violently up into the sky.

As intimidating as the building was, it was dwarfed by the grassy acreage. The grounds were peppered with mature trees, and among them, we could make out shadowy figures stumbling around in the distance. We pulled the van up front. From what we could tell, the facility was deserted. It was getting darker by the minute, yet not a single light shone through the hundreds of barred windows that dotted the front of the building.

"This place gives me the creeps," Celeste offered.

"Me, too," I said. The mysterious figures were getting closer. Zombies in bloodied hospital gowns made their way toward us through the mist. "Look at that. Place has probably been overrun, but at least we know there's a hospital. Let's go take a look."

I grabbed a gun and jumped down from the van. Celeste followed.

"You coming, Alex?" she asked.

"No, I better wait here to keep an eye on Mike," he said.

"Dude, no way. You stay in there you're going to be bait for all those freaks over there," I said.

"But what about Mike? Won't they smell him?" Alex asked.

"Maybe, but he also might become one of them by the time we get back."

The thought of being trapped in the van with Mike was all the motivation Alex needed to grab a gun and join us.

I put my hand on Alex's shoulder. "Look, pal, you were really brave back there at the storage depot. You saved my life *again* when you pulled me out of that mess. You got this, man. Fire up that laser, and let's go torch some freaks."

"All right," Alex said with a sheepish grin. He stepped back and activated his weapon. The laser shot out a good ten feet right between Celeste and me.

"Be careful, Alex," Celeste said, stepping away from the beam. "We better keep our lasers short. We don't want to hurt each other."

29.

We tiptoed into the building, expecting to find ghouls at every turn. Instead, we found ourselves exploring the annals of an abandoned insane asylum. The rooms were mostly empty save for an occasional antediluvian restraint table bolted to the floor, which was littered with brittle plaster that had broken free from the crumbling walls. At first, we moved slowly through the pitch-black rooms, with only the warm glow of the lasers to guide our path. After failing to run into a zombie for a good ten minutes, we started moving faster and faster until we reached the end of the western wing.

"This is weird," I said.

"I know. They couldn't have just packed everything up and left," Celeste said.

"Even if they did, the building wouldn't be in shambles."

"Perhaps the hospital is located in the other wing," Alex suggested.

"I hope so. We better go find out," I said.

We worked our way back toward the other wing. As we walked through the lobby at the center of the building, the clock struck the hour. The thundering bell rattled our bones. We all took a combative stance as if we were under attack, then stood and laughed at the absurdity of the moment. When the clock stopped chiming, the reverberating echo was replaced by howling emanating from somewhere beneath us.

"You hear that?" Celeste asked.

"I do," I said. "Where's it coming from?"

"I don't know."

We stood in place, listening carefully before we moved toward the source of the sound. The wailing led us to towering white drapes that appeared to be covering a very large window. I grabbed the cloth and yanked it back, unveiling a door that was slightly ajar.

"A secret passage," Alex whispered.

"Come on . . . follow me," I said, putting my hand on the door.

"Why?" Alex cried. "We know what's in there."

"We're here to find the hospital, right?"

"Yes, but—"

"If they're trying to stop the outbreak, then what's the one thing they need to have in the hospital?"

"Patients."

"Bingo. Let's go."

I pulled the door back and leapt into the doorway, ready for anything. Instead of zombies, I found a dimly lit stairwell.

"Okay, let's go down. Careful with those lasers behind me, okay?" They nodded.

There weren't more than twenty stairs. At the bottom, they met a concrete hallway that ran to the left. I stood at the corner, my back to the wall, and waited for my companions to catch up. Once they did, I spun around into the hallway. A crowd of zombies at the other end of the hall had their backs to us. They were gathered around a large steel door, screaming and scratching at it in agony. Most wore gowns, but some were soldiers, and others wore the uniforms of medical personnel. Alex opened fire abruptly with his machine gun, which immediately got the ghouls' attention and sent them running toward us. Alex turned and ran back up the stairs, and Celeste and I followed. I looked behind as I rounded the corner and saw what I thought was a face peering through the viewing window on the other side of the door. When I got to the top of the stairs, I slammed the door shut, and then stood panting with my back against it.

"What was that, Alex?" I inquired.

"I don't know. Fighting?"

"Like the enthusiasm, buddy, but you can't be going all Rambo on us. We need to work together."

"What's Rambo?"

"*Of course.* It means wild . . . commando, you know? We need to work as a team."

"Got it."

"There are a lot of them down there," Celeste said.

"I know, and we're going to have to take care of them because there's somebody on the other side of that door."

"How do you know?" Alex asked.

"I saw someone looking through the window."

"I didn't see anyone. How do you know it wasn't one of them?"

"Because, I just know. Besides, why would they all be jonesing to get in there if all there was, was a freak on the other side?"

"He has a point, Alex."

The zombies had followed us up the stairs, and now they were going to work on our door.

"All right, Al, you get the door, and Celeste and I will do the honors," I said.

We readied our lasers, and as soon as Alex pulled the handle, we made quick work of the zombies on the other side. Blood, brains, and entrails saturated the carpeted steps.

We walked gingerly among the carnage careful to avoid still-moving torsos and heads.

When we reached the bottom of the stairs, several zombies were still clawing at the other door. A man behind the window waved at us. We returned the gesture and then pulled back around the corner.

"I guess they weren't ready to give up on him," Celeste whispered.

"I think we should sneak up behind them and take them out," I said, "but we have to use our bayonets cause we don't want the lasers hurting that guy on the other side."

"They won't cut through that steel," she said.

"I know, but what about the glass?"

She nodded.

"No shooting either, Al. Look, there aren't many more of them than there are of us, so we should be fine. Let's move quickly before they know we're here."

We raced down the hallway with our weapons at the ready. Only one zombie heard us coming so I charged in his direction and thrust my bayonet into his eye. Celeste stabbed her target in the back of the head and then hit another attacker with the butt of her rifle and finished him off once he fell to the ground. Alex made an instant kill to the back of the head as well, but he was too overcome by the experience to react quickly to the creature next to his target. It turned and grabbed him by the shoulders, but I thrust my bayonet up underneath its chin before it had a chance to bite him.

With our enemies vanquished, we had a moment to pause. Alex was as white as a ghost.

"You did great, buddy," I said. He nodded slightly. "Looks like I still owe you one."

As I patted him on the shoulder, Celeste noticed the dried blood on my sleeve.

"Royce, are you injured?" she asked.

"Where? Oh, that? Nooo, that's just from when I was helping Mike."

"Oh, good."

Dodging that bullet made me anxious and self-aware. I noticed that I was sweating profusely. I told myself that it was just adrenaline from the fight, but I couldn't be sure.

30.

The man on the other side of the door struggled to force it open against the bodies lying on the ground. We dragged them out of the way and were greeted by a tall, gaunt man in an ill-fitting lab coat that hung loosely on his wiry frame. His hair was dark and curly, and he wore thin-rimmed glasses that he pushed tightly against the top of his nose.

"Am I glad to see you!" He beamed. "Here, come in. Shut the door in case there are more of them out there."

We walked down a flight of stairs and entered a lab eerily similar to the one in New York. The white room was the size of a high school gymnasium with advanced machinery dotting the floor and five large metal gurneys positioned evenly across the center of the room. Three doors ran along one wall, and a massive metal pole stretched from floor to ceiling on the other side of the room.

"I surmise that you weren't sent by the government," the man said.

"Definitely not," I replied.

"How did you even know about this place?"

"We have a friend. He worked in a communication center, and he picked up on things. He's injured; we're hoping you can help him."

"How bad is it?"

"Pretty bad."

"Has he been bitten?"

"Yes."

"Well, as you can see, I can't do anything for that."

"Please, just do whatever you can. Can we bring him down?"

"Certainly. Where is he?"

"He's out front. In the van."

"Okay, here's what I need you to do. Drive your vehicle around the back of the building until you find a cement patio without any furniture on it. Park the van on the patio and honk your horn."

"Um, okay . . ."

"Now get going. If your friend has been bitten, we don't have much time."

31.

The zombies must have smelled Mike, because several were pounding on the door at the back of the van.

"You think that means he's still alive?" Alex asked.

"Let's hope so. If we gotta take him out, just be careful with the food," I said. "Shall I do the honors?"

"Why certainly," Celeste replied, curtsying.

I extended my laser as far as it would go and then snuck around the side of the van. Once I was alongside the zombies, I held the laser above my head and swung straight down like I was chopping wood. This stroke prevented any damage to the van, and it chopped the majority of them right in half.

"Did you guys see that?"

"I like your handiwork," Celeste said, placing her hand on my arm and running it gently across my back as she walked around me to strike a zombie.

My laser had missed the zombie's head and it was trying to get up on one arm and leg. Celeste fired a round into its head, and Alex used his bayonet to finish off another crawling in a circle on the other side of the van.

"You're starting to get the hang of this, aren't you?" I asked Alex.

"It's scary, but it's kind of fun," he said.

"When in Rome, right? Let's see how Mike is doing," I said and swung open the back door of the van.

Mike was lying right where we had left him.

"Okay, let's get him in there," Celeste said.

She climbed into the center of the cab, and Alex sat next to her in the passenger seat. I drove around the building searching for the patio.

"I don't think he's breathing," Celeste said.

"Get your gun ready and keep a close eye on him," I said. "We don't want him sneaking up on us like Carson."

"I don't see what the point of this is," Alex said. "You heard him yourself, he can't cure him."

"He can't if he doesn't try. Medicine is amazing these days, right? What if healing the wounds before he turns stops the virus?"

"I suppose, but I'd be surprised if he hasn't tried that before."

"Well, let's find out," I said as I pulled up onto the patio. I put the van in park and honked the horn.

"Why do you think he has us out here anyway?" Celeste asked.

"Beats me."

As I spoke, the ground shifted. The patio moved slowly downward. When it stopped moving, we were inside the lab. The man in the lab coat waved us forward, and I drove the van off the patio onto the floor. Behind us, the piston returned the patio to the surface.

"Where is he?" the man asked.

"He's in the back," I said.

He rolled a gurney over to the back of the van, and we pulled Mike out and placed him on top of it.

"What's his name?" the man asked.

"Mike," I said.

"I'm Dr. Trowbridge."

"Thanks for helping us out. I'm Royce, this is Celeste, and that handsome specimen there is Alex."

"Very nice to meet you all. Now, your friend here, errr, Mike, is in pretty bad shape. He looks like he's going to turn soon, and I'm going to have to restrain him, okay?"

"Of course."

Dr. Trowbridge stepped on a lever beneath the gurney, and restraints lashed out across Mike's body. He wheeled Mike over to a counter where medical utensils were arranged neatly in a row. He cut off Mike's clothes to expose his wounds. Next, he opened a cabinet and pulled out the same machine Dr. Feng had used to heal the laceration on my arm. He went to work on Mike's wounds, and within fifteen minutes, the skin on his legs, minus the bloodstains, looked as if the injuries had happened long ago. Once he finished with Mike's legs, Dr. Trowbridge took the tourniquet off his triceps and then cleaned and treated the wound.

"There we go," Dr. Trowbridge said. "Anyone else have wounds that need tending to?"

We all shook our heads, and I placed my arm nervously behind my back.

"Well, then, I'm going to inject him with a dose of an antivirus that I've been working on. So far three of the individuals we've injected haven't turned," Dr. Trowbridge said, before retrieving a large needle that he stabbed directly into Mike's heart.

"Where are the three guys who didn't turn?" I asked.

"Two were treated at other facilities."

"And the third?"

"You're looking at him. I was bitten on the arm while restraining a patient here before we were overrun. I treated the wound, took the antiviral, and the disease never progressed. The virus is in my blood, but it's dormant . . . completely inactive."

"How many people have you treated with the antiviral?" Alex asked.

"Hundreds. It's no magic bullet," he said, and then paused and smiled. "Of course, you don't need me to tell you that."

"But how did you even get here?" Alex asked. "I didn't know American doctors were allowed to work alongside the Chinese."

"If they need your expertise, they'll put it to use."

"What's yours?" Celeste asked.

"Immunology and bioterrorism."

"So this is some kind of top-secret facility?" I asked.

"Yes, it is. This is ground zero for countermeasures every time there is an attack. This one, I must say, is brilliant—a virus that ensures it spreads by turning the host against its own species. It's practically unstoppable, and I think it will finally end the war. If we can just stay alive until our troops reclaim the territory, we're going to be free men and women again."

"This wasn't an attack," Alex said.

"I highly doubt that," Dr. Trowbridge countered.

"No, really, it wasn't. I was there at the facility in New York when the first patients became infected. I worked closely with them. They all had the virus in their blood. It mutated, and that's what caused the outbreak."

"Really? That's very interesting. Still, that doesn't mean this wasn't an attack. The virus could have mutated by design."

"We know it wasn't an attack because all of the patients had the virus in their blood before the war began."

"What?" Dr. Trowbridge looked at Alex incredulously. "And how would you know that?"

"Because they were cryogenically frozen when the war started. All four of them. It wasn't until we reanimated them that the virus mutated and the outbreak started."

"That's incredible. I didn't think cryogenic reanimation was possible."

"Neither did I until I worked in the lab where they perfected the procedure. It worked beautifully on the first patient, but the next three broke out in fever. They turned quickly, and no one was ready for what they became. It spread quickly."

"You say three turned. What happened to the fourth patient? Was he or she eaten?"

"Royce is the fourth patient. He and I escaped together."

Dr. Trowbridge turned and looked at me with piqued interest. "Well, well, well, a living, breathing cryonic right here in my lab. I am truly honored."

"You won't be once you get to know me," I said with a wink.

"What year were you frozen?"

"Twenty-ten."

"Oh my, I was just a teenager then. Do you remember Eminem? I used to love listening to Eminem."

"Yes, I remember. My son listens to him."

"Listens?"

"Well," I laughed, "probably not anymore. He's older than I am now."

"And why did Royce survive?" Dr. Trowbridge asked Alex.

"That is a very good question. He also has the virus in his blood, but it didn't mutate."

"I'd love to run some tests on you, Royce."

"Um, okay, but can we eat first? I'm starving."

32.

We pulled a bag of rice from the back of the truck and cooked over the intense flame of a small, candle-shaped torch that reminded me of the Bunsen burners from my high school chemistry class. The lab had glass bowls to eat from and measuring utensils that served as spoons. With some warm meat and vegetables on top of the rice, the meal wasn't half bad.

"This is incredible," Dr. Trowbridge said with a groan of pleasure.

"How long has it been?" Celeste asked.

"Ah, let's see. Two days now since the food ran out," he said between mouthfuls. "How'd you come across these rations?"

"We raided a depot in Silver Spring," she said.

"That's impressive. You are some real warriors, I take it."

"The military wasn't there. Well, they were, but they were all infected. They all seem to have it now, at least as far as we've seen."

Dr. Trowbridge stopped eating. "I see. I didn't realize it was spreading that quickly. I wonder if it's made it over to the other side yet?"

"I don't know."

"This virus has the ability to wipe out the entire human race, and here I thought living under Chinese rule was the worst that could happen."

Everything he said was true. All we could do was nod solemnly.

33.

That night, we slept in the doctors' living quarters, a concrete room at the back of the lab with small plastic cabinets among several twin beds. We were safe, comfortable, and fed for the first time since the outbreak, and we slept soundly. The next morning, we had scarcely finished breakfast when Mike started writhing against the straps holding him to the gurney. Dr. Trowbridge ran over.

"He's turned. I'm sorry."

Mike growled and snapped at Dr. Trowbridge, who shined a light in his eyes.

"We're going to have to do something about him," I said.

"I'll do it," Alex volunteered.

"You sure, buddy?" I asked.

"Certain. I feel bad that the two of you have had to pull all the weight so far. If it wasn't for Mike, I doubt you both would have survived the depot. Now that he's gone, you're going to need me more than ever. If this is the world we're living in, it's time for me to embrace it."

Alex picked up a gun and walked over to speak with Dr. Trowbridge, who pointed at a door on the far side of the room. They pushed Mike's gurney toward the door, and Alex took it inside. A short time later, Alex emerged, his clothes splattered with fresh blood.

34.

"Can I take your blood now?" Dr. Trowbridge asked.

"Sure, doc," I said, looking nervously at Alex and Celeste, who were sitting against the side of the van, talking. "You think we could do it somewhere private?"

"A squeamish one, are you?"

"Only at the sight of my own blood."

"Okay. We can go into that room there, and that way, if you pass out on me, you won't be embarrassed in front of your friends."

We entered the room adjacent to the one where Alex put Mike out of his misery. I sat down in a chair the doctor had positioned alongside a table, and he laid a syringe and several vials next to me.

"Um, doc."

"Yes, Royce."

"I'm not really squeamish. I have something that I want to show you, but you can't tell the others about it, okay?"

"All right."

I rolled back my right sleeve and removed the bandage to reveal the wound on my arm. The doctor held my arm and leaned in close to inspect it.

"I take it this is a bite."

"Yes, doctor."

"And it isn't from your lady friend out there?"

"Who, Celeste? No," I said, my face turning a slight shade of red.

"Have you run a fever?"

"I worked up quite a sweat when we fought our way in here, but other than that I've felt fine."

He pulled a small metal cylinder out of his pocket. It was one of those hologram devices that Dr. Feng had shown me in New York. An image of my body emerged above it. "Nope, you aren't running a fever. When were you bitten?"

"The same time as Mike. Bastards got me when my laser went out."

"Well, I have some good news for you."

"You do?"

"I do. You most definitely do not have the virus. You would have turned by now, or you'd at least have quite a high fever. Though, I shouldn't say you don't have the virus. I'll draw some blood to be certain, but as Alex informed me, you already had it in your system."

Dr. Trowbridge drew some blood from my arm and left the room. He returned about five minutes later.

"That was fast," I said.

"I have some even better news for you. I thought you might have had a different mutated strain in your blood than those who were infected, but I don't see that. Besides, the bite exposed you to the strain that's causing the outbreak. It's in your blood, but your immune system has things under control. Long story short—you're immune."

A wave of relief washed over me, but then I started thinking. "Why me, doc? What makes me immune?"

"That is the ultimate question. I have a hunch, but first let's take care of that arm."

35.

After Dr. Trowbridge healed my arm, he took me back into the lab to speak with Alex and Celeste.

"Find anything interesting?" Alex asked.

"Very interesting, indeed," Dr. Trowbridge replied. "The virus in Royce's blood is the same as in mine, but his immune system is keeping it in check."

"So he's had it all along, just like the other cryonics?"

"As far as I can tell."

"Well, how else would he get it?" Celeste asked.

"Let me handle that one, doc," I said. "Um, look, guys, there's something I've been keeping from you. I got bit yesterday. It happened when my laser went kaput."

"Why didn't you tell us?" Celeste asked, her eyes turning fiery.

"I figured you two had enough to worry about, and, well, I was afraid."

"Afraid?" Alex asked.

"Yes, afraid. Afraid of turning into one of those freaks."

"Is that why you brought us here, so that you could get treatment?"

"Yes and no. I mean, what were we supposed to do? We had two wounded soldiers. Listen, I was going to put a bullet in my brain as soon as the fever started. I just wanted a chance . . . a chance for all of us to survive together."

"And how are Alex and I supposed to trust you now that we know this? It's life and death out there, every single moment of every day."

"You and Al should trust me because your friendship is all I've got in this twisted world. And my intentions were good. Alex told me I was probably already exposed to the virus just like the other cryonics, and I didn't want you two to get worked up over nothing. I didn't know what else to do. At least I came clean about it."

"I don't know what to make of you, Royce Bruyere."

Celeste walked off in a huff and sat in the front seat of the van. Alex went over to console her. The doctor had left the conversation when things got personal, so I was left alone to sulk.

36.

Alex came over and sat with me. He'd been talking to Celeste in the van for quite a while.

"It'll blow over soon," he said. "She never holds grudges for long."

"I hope so. I don't have enough friends to have any of them mad at me."

"Don't worry. She'll get past it."

"I take it the two of you were an item once?"

"Who me? Us?" Alex laughed nervously and his cheeks turned beet red. "No, we're just old friends."

"She's quite a catch, Al. You want me to put in a good word for ya?"

"Like that will help."

"Touché, my forlorn friend, touché. Say, how does she know my last name?"

"I told her. She asked me, and I told her. She talks about you a lot."

Now I was the one blushing.

37.

"Guys, can you come over here for a minute?" Dr. Trowbridge called out from across the room.

Dr. Trowbridge sat in front of what from a distance looked like a large computer screen. Once I got close, I realized the image was projected in front of him into thin air. He controlled the device with his hands, waving them to drag new images onto the screen.

"Do you have Internet on this thing?" I asked.

"Internet." He chuckled and winked at Alex. "I haven't heard that term in a long time. Unfortunately, there's no outside access. This is a closed system, similar to what you would call an Intranet. You can imagine the Chinese don't want us accessing outside information."

Celeste walked up behind me. "What's going on?" she asked.

"Dr. Trowbridge was just about to show us something," Alex replied.

"Look at this," he said. Two case files with profile shots of Chinese men in uniform were side by side on the screen. "These are the histories of the two soldiers I thought had responded to the antivirus, *but* after coming across Royce here, I'm beginning to think differently."

"How so?" Alex asked.

"Well, for starters, Royce wasn't exposed to the antivirus yet he didn't contract the disease. The low hit rate for the antivirus already suggested either it wasn't working at all or it lacked the efficacy to serve as a viable solution. So with the antivirus out, just one course of inquiry remained—commonalities among the individuals who failed to contract the disease."

"Got all this, Al?" I asked. Alex nodded. "Good because I might need to copy your notes after class."

Dr. Trowbridge smiled. "It'll all make sense in a moment, Royce. Both these men fought in the oil wars in Africa, which means they had an extensive round of immunizations that most soldiers aren't exposed to. See this here? Polio, typhoid, smallpox, hepatitis, meningitis, HIV . . . the list goes on and on."

Dr. Trowbridge paused, and they all looked at me.

"Oh, I get it. You all are funny. You're waiting for me to react to the HIV vaccine. Sorry to disappoint you, but I'm not going to jump up and down like a chimp just because you cured AIDS. In case you haven't noticed, you have a machine that can seal up a freaking gash in my arm the size of a bratwurst in seconds. Of course, you've cured AIDS."

"Well then, my background doesn't help us much. Due to my work with infectious diseases, I've been vaccinated against everything under the sun. Which brings me to you, Royce. I'm willing to bet that you were born sometime in the nineteen sixties, correct?"

"Yessir, nineteen sixty-three."

"And those poor souls in New York, the ones who started this whole thing. In what years were they born?"

Alex spoke up. "Let's see . . . Barry was born in 1973, Elliott in 1981, and Janet was 1993."

"I knew it!" Trowbridge yelped, thrusting both arms into the air. Then he started speaking to himself in a subdued voice, "Andrew, you clever son of a bitch, you did it."

"Hey, doc, before you break your arm patting yourself on the back you mind telling us what the hell you're talking about?" I asked.

"Of course, I'm sorry. It's the smallpox. They stopped vaccinating for it in 1972, which means you were vaccinated for it, and the other cryonics were not. Soldiers serving in Africa received it because there had been an outbreak there before the war, and I was vaccinated because I handle it here in the lab. It's the only thing that separates the four of us from the rest of the population."

"But why would a smallpox vaccine stop the virus?" Alex asked. "Back in New York, we determined the origin virus was JCV."

"Good question. Apparently, the mutated virus is similar enough to smallpox that the vaccine prepares the body to defend against it. We didn't think it was similar enough for this to happen, but by God, it works! Think of it this way. The smallpox vaccine doesn't actually contain the smallpox virus. It uses a vaccinia virus that is similar enough to smallpox that its presence equips the body's defenses for the real thing. That vaccine also prepares the body for this virus."

"So it's a cure then," I said.

"It isn't a cure. It's only a vaccine, but it may be able to lessen the infection if given soon enough after exposure."

"How soon?"

"That I don't know. The sooner the better."

"What about the ones wandering around outside? Can we give it to them?"

"No, there's no curing them. They're already dead."

"Well, how do you explain them wandering around, attacking people, and stuff when the virus has already killed them?"

"That . . . defies explanation. It may very well be the hand of God clearing the Earth of man's transgressions."

38.

"This will greatly increase your chances of survival," Dr. Trowbridge said as he pricked Alex repeatedly with the smallpox vaccine.

"If it works," Alex pointed out.

"Indeed. *If* it works."

Celeste had received the vaccine first, and was now sitting on a chair holding her shoulder. As I watched them get vaccinated, I was overcome by the incredible power of the opportunity that we'd been given. We were very likely the only people in the world who knew how to beat the disease. I thought of my wife and son back in San Diego. They needed to know about this, and I needed to see them. I needed to go home.

"You're awful quiet over there," Celeste coaxed.

"Just thinking, that's all."

"Thinking about what?"

"About what we do now."

"What we do now? We stay here until the food runs out," Alex chimed in. "This is a safe place. We could even build a barricade upstairs and spread out a little."

"What about the people back home?" I wondered.

"Back home?" Celeste asked.

"You know . . . out West. The people who are free. Are we going to just let them die of this?"

"You're making a lot of assumptions there. The entire US military is set up along the front. Nothing is going to make it past that," Alex said.

"You said the same thing when we were in the city. The Chinese military was going to come and clear the streets any minute. Remember that?"

Alex grew quiet.

"How are they doing against the freaks so far, Alex?"

"What if I'm incorrect?" Dr. Trowbridge asked. "What if the vaccine doesn't work?"

"Then at least we'll know we tried. That's a lot better than sitting here holed up like a bunch of cowards."

"I'll do it," Celeste broke in solemnly.

"Do what?" Alex asked.

"I'll be the guinea pig. Inject me with the virus, and we'll see if the vaccine works."

"No, Celeste! Please?" Alex begged.

"Do you know how many people we could save? Our whole country. We could save our whole country if this works."

"And if it doesn't?" I asked.

"Then that's my choice. I don't want to live like this—trapped in a basement, fearing for my life every time I step outside. This isn't living. This is captivity. I've been in captivity long enough. I want to be free."

Silence filled the room.

Never one to bite my tongue, I spoke first. "Can you do it, doc?"

"Of course, I can inject her with tainted blood, but I'm uncertain if I want this on my conscience."

"You haven't been outside yet, doc. You're going to have far worse things on your conscience just trying to stay alive."

39.

Early that evening, Dr. Trowbridge caved under the pressure. Since the smallpox virus starts working immediately, he went ahead and injected Celeste with a small vial of tainted blood. I couldn't believe how calm she was about the whole thing. I'd never seen such courage.

She chatted with us late into the evening and then lay down to sleep. Alex, Dr. Trowbridge, and I stayed up through the night, fidgeting nervously like expectant fathers stuck in the waiting room. Celeste was an early riser, so when she didn't wake up by nine a.m. we knew something was wrong. By ten, she was running a fever, and Dr. Trowbridge woke her up to give her fluids and draw blood.

"How you doing, kid?" I asked.

She looked me in the eye and drew me close with her index finger. "I want you to be the one to do it," she said. "Don't let Alex see it. He's been through enough already."

"I'll do nothing of the sort." I smiled. "You just hang in there. You're gonna beat this."

40.

"You gotta do something for her, doc," I pleaded.

Dr. Trowbridge was off at his workbench running tests on Celeste's blood. It was nearly one p.m., and her fever was growing worse by the hour. She was in a deep sleep, lying on a bed we'd brought out into the middle of the lab. Alex sat alongside her and held her hand.

"There's nothing I can do," he explained. "I can inject her so full of drugs that her blood will curdle, but that won't do a thing. It's up to her body now. Her immune system has to beat this thing."

41.

At six p.m. Celeste was still sleeping, and Alex had retreated to the doctor's quarters to rest. I sat next to her wondering if my selfishness had once again reared its ugly head. I wanted to save my family, sure, but the future of our country was riding on this cure as well. At least that's what I told myself while I listened to Alex crying himself to sleep.

"I'm going to get some rest as well," Dr. Trowbridge said. "I think it's time we restrain her."

"Okay, Andy. You go. I'll take care of it."

Dr. Trowbridge patted my neck, then turned and headed back into his sleeping quarters. Celeste looked beautiful lying there, even though her skin was pale and clammy. Her ravenesque hair and full lips were reminiscent of Snow White's peaceful slumber. I noticed she was no longer sweating profusely, and I wondered if she'd soon be writhing in pain and moaning like the others had before they turned.

"Why did you have to be so God damned brave?" I whispered in her ear. I was angry with her, but only because I was angry with myself. "We could have made it out there—all of us. We could have gone out West and been free."

I stood and leaned forward with my hands on the edge of the bed. I was overcome by sadness and shame. My head drooped low, and my eyes welled with tears. I felt deeply responsible for her death. I was selfish for bringing her to the hospital in the first place, and selfish for trying to persuade them to head West.

"I am *so* sorry," I said, closing my eyes to fight back the tears.

That's when I felt her hands clutch my throat. My eyes sprang open. Celeste's teeth were clenched, and her eyes were wide and maniacal. I looked to my left and right, searching desperately for something to smash her with, but found nothing. And that's when it hit me. Her eyes—they weren't glazed and bloodshot like the others. They looked normal, even human. Before I had a chance to react to this realization, her hands went limp on my collarbone, and she burst out laughing.

"Did you miss me, you big baby?" she teased.

"You are pure evil," I said, pushing her hands off me. "I really thought you were done."

"Awww, Mr. Funny Man doesn't like it when the shoe's on the other foot, does he?"

"I guess not."

"You deserve it, and you know it."

"I guess so. What the hell is going on with you? Are you all right?"

"How long have I been sleeping?"

"Since this morning when we last spoke."

"Honestly, I feel pretty good now. I think I might have kicked it."

And kicked it she had.

42.

Alex was overjoyed to have Celeste back. Dr. Trowbridge, too, though I think hc was more excited about being the first person to cure the disease. Celeste regained her strength quickly, and in a couple of days, the four of us were packed and ready to go. We planned to head west and find a way to sneak across the front. If we wanted to deliver the cure and give our soldiers the upper hand, we needed to get to the US side before the plague did.

We checked out the abandoned homes in Weston. I felt like an intruder. If you ignored the dust and decay, it looked like the families might return at any moment. Breakfasts were spread out neatly on kitchen tables, and newspapers all bore the same tragic date, Thursday, March 13, 2036. Pictures hung on the wall of those who had lost their freedom. Some beds were neatly made while others looked as if the sleeping occupants had been dragged out of them.

The best thing we found inside the houses was the bedding. Sleeping in the back of the van was going to be uncomfortable with it loaded with supplies. Bottled water was also a great find, as it saved us the trouble of having to find a water source and boil it ourselves. The only other things we brought with us from the homes were flashlights, a hatchet, and a pair of binoculars.

43.

We left Weston in late morning and made it into central Kentucky just before dark. Driving around the cities was pitifully slow as the roadways were littered with the vehicles of those who had attempted to flee only to get bottlenecked by military roadblocks. Most vehicles had broken windows. The occupants' mangled corpses lay nearby. Those who hadn't been dragged to the pavement were splattered across the insides of their cars. Cars that had left the line of traffic were riddled with bullet holes. It was clear the Chinese knew the outbreak was coming and tried to keep people inside the city. Such an incredible waste given that the roadblocks were also overrun. Soldiers' bodies were strewn among piles of chopped-up zombie corpses. We wondered whether the soldiers had been killed because their lasers ran out or they were overcome by a never-ending mass of fearless attackers.

We drove into the countryside well west of Louisville, and decided we wouldn't stop until we hadn't seen a ghoul for at least half an hour. That would leave a pretty good cushion between us and the zombies lumbering along the roadway. In the end, it didn't matter. We hadn't been asleep for two hours before pounding on the outside of the van woke us up. We decided to keep on driving. We drove in shifts: two slept, one drove, and the other watched for zombies and our driver falling asleep.

We approached eastern St. Louis shortly before dawn, and our surroundings changed dramatically. Abandoned towns and paved roads gave way to bombed-out military bunkers and barbed wire barriers lining the rutted dirt roads that crisscrossed the landscape. The zombies walking aimlessly outside our windows no longer included Chinese civilians and Americans. They were all Chinese soldiers.

"We better stop," Dr. Trowbridge insisted. "We don't want to enter the front until daylight. It's safer that way."

"Why?" Alex asked.

"It'll be easier for the Chinese to capture us if we don't know where they are."

"How are we going to get past them?" I asked.

"I'm not certain, but we'll find a way."

44.

We waited until an hour after sunrise, then entered eastern St. Louis carefully. After nearly a decade of war, the city was in ruins. Most of the buildings had been toppled or gutted by explosions. Others had been reconstructed as bunkers hidden beneath the rubble. The binoculars proved essential as we scouted each section of the city's remains before determining that it was safe to enter. The closer we moved to the river, the fewer zombies we saw.

"Where the hell are they?" I asked. "I thought you said there were millions of soldiers stationed along the river."

"There were," Alex replied. "I don't know where they went. If they've succumbed to the disease, they sure aren't here."

Alex was right. There weren't enough zombies considering the massive number of Chinese soldiers stationed in the area. Then we saw the river. Things started to make sense. Massive craters lined our side of the shoreline. Pieces of Chinese soldiers were everywhere. Yapping heads flopped about, and torsos dragged themselves along the ground. Zombies, not soldiers, had been annihilated.

"Did you notice how all of the bunkers were empty?" Dr. Trowbridge asked.

"Yes, and the vehicles, too," Alex said.

"What do you think happened?" Celeste asked.

Dr. Trowbridge curled his hand in front of his mouth. He studied the river as if it held the answers.

"They wanted to get across," he said.

"The freaks?" I asked.

"Exactly. When enough of them had succumbed to the disease, they didn't have a food source on this side of the river. When they saw the soldiers on the other side, they lined the shoreline."

"What soldiers on the other side? I don't see anybody," I said.

"They must have been aware of the disease. Perhaps they retreated after bombing this side. No need to monitor the front when your enemy is already dead."

"I think you're right about them wanting to get to the other side," I said. "Look in the river. See that? Oh, there's another one. And right up there, there's three more." I pointed at the bloated corpses twisting and turning in the river as the current dragged them downstream.

"What do you think is happening on the other side?" Celeste asked.

"I'm not certain, but we better go and have a look."

45.

We searched several empty bunkers and found two gun chargers, a rocket launcher, and ammunition. Then we drove along the waterfront and found the hull of an old apartment building that still had the fire escape attached. We parked the van underneath the iron staircase and climbed to the top of the ladder. Dr. Trowbridge and I used the binoculars to scan the city on the other side of the river. Just like on our side, St. Louis was in ruins. Even the Gateway Arch was destroyed. All that remained were two mutilated stubs protruding from the ground. Through the binoculars, I saw groups of US soldiers roaming the streets. When I focused in closer, it was clear they'd turned.

"You see them?" I asked Dr. Trowbridge.

"Yes, I see them. Sorry, everyone, but it looks like our soldiers have succumbed to the virus as well. I don't think we should cross here. There's too many of them."

As far as we could see in both directions, the massive eight-lane Poplar Street Bridge was the only bridge that still spanned the waterway. The others had been blown to bits. I could see a massive barricade in the center of the bridge and a vast horde of US soldier zombies roaming the other side.

"I don't think we could cross here even if we wanted to. If we did make it across, we'd never make it through the city," I suggested.

"Do you think there are other bridges intact?" Alex asked.

"There won't be many, I know that," Dr. Trowbridge replied.

"Um, guys, looks like we have a problem," Celeste said, looking down at the van, which was surrounded by several dozen zombies. They groaned and held their arms in the air as if they might be able to reach us.

"I guess we attracted them by coming up here," I said.

"What did you expect? They can see us from half a mile away," Alex grumbled. He started climbing down the fire escape.

"Geeze, what's gotten into him?"

We all had our rifles, but Alex led the charge. He jumped down from the bottom rung to the van, turned on his laser, and dispatched the majority of them before Celeste could even get her laser going. Once she did, Celeste finished off the remaining ones. We followed them down and got in the van.

"Boy, you weren't kidding about pulling your own weight, were you?" I prodded Alex. He smiled back at me and shook his head.

46.

We drove north along the eastern edge of the river, searching for a bridge to cross. We were several miles north of the city and still hadn't found one intact when the shockwave from a massive explosion rattled the van. Alex slammed on the brakes, and we all leaped out. A massive mushroom cloud rose over the city on the other side of the river. Another explosion detonated a mile or two closer to us. The shockwave that quickly followed knocked us to the ground and blew the windows out of the van. That explosion was followed by another and another. We sat silent on the ground, watching in awe as four bulbous burnt sienna mushroom clouds crowded the sky above the city.

"The Chinese are using nukes again?" I yelped. The other three were much calmer. War was desensitizing.

"No, those are conventional weapons," Dr. Trowbridge responded. "If they were using nukes, they wouldn't need four bombs."

"We would also be covered in radiation burns by now," Alex added.

"Why are they bombing the city? Are they retaliating for getting wiped out along the river?"

"The Americans are doing it. They're trying to contain the plague. That's why they aren't using nukes—they don't want to sully their own soil," Dr. Trowbridge explained.

"Well, thank God we didn't try to cross that bridge," I said.

"Indeed."

47.

We drove a good hundred miles northwest along the river. Every bridge, large and small, was destroyed. On both sides of the river were bombed-out bunkers, half-submerged hulls of sunken ships, wandering zombie soldiers, and abandoned vehicles. Things grew more desolate the further we traveled.

"Stop the car, Alex," I said.

"What's the matter?" Celeste asked.

"Look, we need to cross this river, and if the last hundred miles haven't taught you anything . . . they blew out all the bridges. So, unless we're going to head back to St. Louis to become cannon fodder, I think we need to swim across."

"Swim across?" Alex gasped.

"Either that or we can drive all the way to Canada searching for a bridge."

"What about the van and the food?" Alex asked.

"We'll just have to resupply on the other side."

"You'd think there'd be a boat around here somewhere," Celeste observed.

"Would you let your enemy across the river keep one afloat?" Dr. Trowbridge asked. "I think Royce is right. The further we go, the more time we're giving the outbreak to spread. We need to get the cure in the right hands before it's too late."

"Where though?" Alex asked. "Where are we going to be able to swim across?"

"I saw a place back at the last bend that had a big shallow sand bar on the other side. If we swim across there, it can't be more than a few hundred yards to the bar. Once we reach it, we can stand and walk the rest of the way. There were some military vehicles near a bunker about a mile south of that. We can drive one of those," I said.

"I'm in," Celeste said.

"How about you, Al?" I asked.

"Let's do it," he said.

48.

We parked the van half a mile north of the bend. We knew it wasn't smart to eat before swimming, but we didn't know when our next meal was going to come. So, we ate a bit, and chugged as much water as we could. Our guns were made out of some lightweight composite material, but still heavy enough that we decided they were all the other three would carry for the swim. I was a strong swimmer so I carried the pair of binoculars. We stripped down to our skivvies so we wouldn't sink under the weight of our waterlogged clothes. Then we strapped the weapons tightly to our backs.

Alex and Dr. Trowbridge looked hilarious in their underwear. Both were ghost white and covered in body hair. The weapons on their backs completed the odd look. Celeste was a different story. I tried to keep my eyes off her, but it was practically impossible. She looked amazing standing there in her government-issue white cotton panties and bra. They looked like they were designed for an eighty-year-old woman, yet she still pulled it off.

"Who knew this big ugly thing would get us this far?" I asked, patting the side of the van. Anything to shift my attention away from Celeste.

"It's a shame we have to leave all of this food behind," she said.

"It is a shame. Though, we just gotta find some friendlies on the other side, and we'll be eating again soon."

The muddy brown water of the Mississippi was far more intimidating once we stood alongside it. We watched carefully as it swirled and pulsed downstream.

"You're all strong enough for this, right?" I asked the crew. They nodded without taking their eyes off the river. "It's going to take you about ten minutes if you keep up your stroke. Try to keep an even pace and your head down. You don't want to spaz for three minutes and then panic because you find that you aren't even halfway across. And don't worry about moving downstream. We're in the perfect position for that as long as you keep your stroke up. If for some reason you can't, go ahead and ditch your gun. We'll find you another one on the other side."

"Why don't we all just ditch our guns?" Alex asked.

"Because it's another mile to those vehicles and you know there's going to be freaks waiting for us on the other side."

We waded into the water as far as we could, took a good long look at each other, and then started swimming. The cool water was refreshing against the summer heat. The weight of the gun wasn't bad at first, either. The water near the shoreline was calm and gentle, and the pressure of the gun on my back just made it a bit harder to get my head above water to breathe. As we swam out into the center of the river, the force of the current increased, and the water grew cold and choppy—a lot choppier than it had looked from shore.

Alex started to panic and tried to get rid of his weapon. He struggled against the straps, splashing about frantically. Celeste and Dr. Trowbridge were keeping a good pace so I told them to keep going. I went after Alex.

"Just calm down, buddy. I'm going to help you out with that," I said while treading water beside him. "Just keep your head up, and I'll get it off you."

I swam around behind him and started working on the straps. I tried to work quickly as we were still drifting downstream and losing valuable time. I almost had the weapon off when I felt a hand grab hold of my hair. I turned. A bloated naked zombie floated in the water. It was on its back and didn't seem to have swimming figured out. I kicked it a few feet away from us. This kept it at bay long enough for me to finish removing Alex's weapon.

"Get going, buddy," I said. "I'll catch up to you in a minute. Remember, head down and stay calm, OK?"

Alex started swimming toward Celeste and Dr. Trowbridge. I swam over to the zombie and stuck Alex's bayonet deep into the skull. The zombie stopped moving and floated downstream behind me, the rifle sticking up into the air. I chuckled at the sight, raised my head high out of the water to see if I could spot any more trouble, and continued swimming.

I caught up to Alex and was crawling alongside him when I heard Celeste scream ahead of us. I caught a glimpse of her arms in the air before she was pulled under. I put my head down and sprinted as fast as I could. When I got there, Dr. Trowbridge was treading water.

"What happened?" I asked.

"I don't know. I think she got caught on something."

Celeste popped up a few feet from us, screamed again, and then disappeared back under the water. I dove straight under and swam in the direction of where she had surfaced. I couldn't see a thing in the murky water, but kept swimming deeper until I felt her hand hit my arm. I grabbed it and pulled my way down her body until I felt the fleshy hands clutching her ankles. I could see the zombie's face. It was fresh (not bloated and decomposing like the one I'd seen floating), and it was holding her tight as it gradually sank to the bottom. I kicked the zombie repeatedly in the face, which had no effect upon its grasp. When we reached the bottom, I searched desperately for something to hit the zombie with but found nothing. I pulled on its fingers until I'd released its grasp. It grabbed me by the arms. I put my feet on its shoulders and pushed myself free. I was desperate for air as I swam upward, and I gasped loudly as soon as my face broke the surface.

"Are you all right?" I asked Celeste, who was treading water.

"I'm fine . . ." she said before coughing up water. "Really, I'm fine."

"Go, you two! Go, go, swim for shore. They don't know how to swim, but it's floating with the current right underneath us. Just get away from here, and I'll go for Alex."

Celeste and Dr. Trowbridge did as I told them. Alex was just ten yards behind us. As I turned to swim toward him, the ghoul beneath me swiped at my ankle.

"Hey, buddy," I said, treading water alongside Alex, "we need to change our course a little bit. There's a freak up there, and he's drifting along underneath the surface—right where you're headed. They can't swim so we need to just adjust course to avoid him. We're going to swim against the current for a little while, okay?"

Alex nodded and spit out water.

"Just count thirty strokes with me against the current, and then we'll head for shore. That'll keep us away from him."

Alex did as I told him. By the time we were within eyeshot of the sandbar, Celeste and Dr. Trowbridge were already standing on it. We were too far away from shore to join them. We watched desperately as we drifted downriver past the sandbar.

"All right, Al, it's time to dig deep. We need to make one last push toward shore before the river gets much wider. Can you do it?" I asked.

"I can do it," he said.

The river opened up quickly, which added a good hundred yards to our swim. By the time we reached the rocky riverbank, we were well past the sandbar and good and scraped up from our rough exit.

49.

"You did good," I said, patting Alex on the back. We sat on the edge of the riverbank, trying to catch our breath.

"But my gun . . . it's gone."

"Aw, don't worry about that. Here, you can take mine."

I took the gun off my back and handed it to Alex. Once we'd had a moment to rest, we walked up a grassy hill near the edge of the shoreline to look for Celeste and Dr. Trowbridge. We could see them in the distance walking toward us. I looked the other way, to see how far we needed to walk to the vehicles. I noticed a bunker hidden in the back of the hillside about fifty yards away.

"Hey, Al, you see that?"

"Yes, yes, I do. Looks like a bunker. Maybe there are some more guns in there. You want to go have a look?"

"Sure, why not."

The bunker had been built with large stones. There was a short, narrow doorway on the right and a tiny window on the left. It was dark, and we couldn't see inside. We crept carefully toward the doorway and stopped about fifteen feet away.

"Careful," I said. "There might be some freaks in there. Better turn on your laser."

"OK."

Alex pushed on the button to retract the bayonet. Nothing happened. He turned the gun sideways and held the button closer to his face, pushing on it repeatedly.

"It's not working," he said.

Zombies in camouflage army uniforms burst out of the door.

"It's not working, it's not working!" he screamed.

"Shoot them!" I yelled.

The zombies were just a few feet away. Alex pointed the gun at them and pulled the trigger. Nothing happened.

"The safety!" I yelled, surveying our surroundings for something to defend myself with.

Alex struggled to find it. I reached over and clicked the safety off. Alex sprayed the front line of attackers with a wild burst of gunfire. It ran across the chests of two before going up into the head of a third and off into the horizon. The head shot took care of that one, but the other two kept coming. I pushed one down, and Alex drove his bayonet into the other's skull. There were more right behind them, and two tackled me to the ground. I pushed one off with my left hand and held the other at bay by the throat. I looked over at Alex. His bayonet was still lodged in the zombie's skull. He tried desperately to pull it out, but it was stuck. As he stood there struggling, three more zombies lumbered around their impaled comrade and took Alex down.

I will never forget Alex's screams. They were so high-pitched, so bloodcurdling that they tore my focus away from the zombie on my left, which bit hard into my rib cage. The rush of pain and my friend's plight made my adrenaline surge. I rolled the zombie laying on top of me into the other and stumbled to my feet. Three zombies crouched over Alex. One tugged morsels of flesh from his neck with its teeth. The other two dug deep into his abdomen, pulled out his intestines, and pushed them clumsily into their mouths.

I stood there in shock watching those horrible creatures devour my closest friend. Alex was silent and no longer moving. He was gone. The two zombies hunting me lunged. I broke free from their outstretched arms. I didn't even look at them; survival no longer mattered. All I wanted was to help my friend, but I couldn't. I stormed over and yanked the rifle from the dead zombie's skull. I blasted a flurry of rounds into the temple of the zombie on my side of Alex's abdomen and another burst into the face of the zombie on the other side. Then I turned to the ghoul eating his neck and drove the bayonet deep into the back of its skull. I put my foot on its back and pulled the bayonet out, then held the gun high above my head and swung it down again. I yelled at the top of my lungs as I repeated this over and over until the head was in so many pieces that I didn't know where to strike. My tunnel vision was so consuming that I didn't realize Celeste and Dr. Trowbridge had run up behind me and killed the two remaining attackers.

"Oh my God . . . oh my God. Alex!" Celeste cried. She knelt beside him and placed her hand gently against his bloodstained face. One by one, her tears splashed onto his forehead.

I fell down into a heap and wept for my fallen friend. He had saved my life so many times, and I was crushed by the realization that I couldn't do the same for him.

50.

Dr. Trowbridge searched the bunker but found only several clips of ammunition. We walked from the bunker to the vehicles in a heavy silence. Celeste and I were devastated, and only moved at Trowbridge's insistence. Through the binoculars, I saw more zombies milling about in the distance. We shambled along in our underwear, our hair still dripping wet. My side ached and bled, but the wound wasn't life-threatening, as my rib cage prevented the bite from going deep.

My companions' lasers had also been ruined by the river. We were broken and vulnerable, moving out in the open with nothing but bayonets and a few clips of ammunition between us and untold numbers of walking dead.

51.

"What a hunk of junk! And no keys, either," Dr. Trowbridge said, slamming the door shut on a Humvee. "They must have retreated as soon as the plague reached this side of the river."

"How do you know that?" I asked.

"Well, first off, there's hardly any of them here, minus the infected we saw back in the city, and second, they left nothing behind but the junk."

To me, the vehicles looked like modern, military-grade Humvees, but I suppose that's because they were built during my lifetime.

"Why would they even have these things?" I asked. "They're old as dirt."

"This war changed everything," he explained. "The military put anything they could get their hands on along the front . . . anything to keep the Chinese from moving west."

"Well, they aren't going west anymore."

"Not alive they aren't," Celeste added.

Her comment was a stark reminder of our duty and the challenge before us. I opened the driver's side door on another Humvee and was relieved to find the key in the ignition. I climbed inside, pushed the gas, and turned the key. The engine rocked and choked before roaring to life.

"Now *this* is my kind of car," I said, leaning my head out the window. "She runs like a champ and has almost a full tank of gas to boot."

"That's good," Dr. Trowbridge said, "because we won't be able to refill the tank."

"Why not?" I asked.

"No gas stations. Just charging stations. Nobody uses fuel anymore except the military and aviators."

"We'll find an airport then. I bet this thing will run on AVGAS."

"Once we make it to Kansas City, maybe. They moved everybody away from the front when the war started so there won't be anything between here and there. Of course, once we get to KC we can probably just get another car. That's assuming . . ."

"The city is overrun?"

"Yes, and if it is, we'll just keep on going."

"Do you think they'll listen to us once we find them?" Celeste asked.

"Who, the military?"

"Whoever."

"We need to find the military, and if we do, they'll listen to me. Somebody there ought to be able to verify my credentials. I worked for them long enough."

"You were in the military?"

"No, just a consultant, but I worked for them exclusively for several years before the war. The Chinese sought me out because of that."

"They trusted you?"

"They had to. I knew our bioterrorism tactics better than anyone. Plus, they threatened me with reeducation if I mislead them. I figured I wasn't going to be any use to our boys back home if that happened, so I played along all these years in the hope that one day I might be able to help the cause. Now with you two . . . that day is here."

"That's heavy, doc. I hope we can find them soon. The longer we take, the more it seems like we're going to find freaks instead of people."

We drove southwest through fallow fields until we found a road that linked up to I-70. We could get there more easily through the city, but we didn't want to go anywhere near it after the bombing. The Humvee was loud and it vibrated wildly, but it felt safe, and it tore right through the uneven terrain.

We barreled down the highway, raising our voices over the road noise.

"I don't know about you two, but this drive will be a lot more comfortable if we can find some clothes," I said. "I'm getting tired of looking at you two in your underwear."

"You're not so hot yourself," Dr. Trowbridge joked.

"How about there?" Celeste asked. She pointed toward fallen soldiers at an abandoned checkpoint.

I stopped the vehicle. "You want to wear their uniforms?"

"Might be all we can find," Dr. Trowbridge said. "Very little between here and KC."

"But we found all kinds of stuff in Weston."

"This wasn't that kind of evacuation. It was a relocation. People had time to collect their belongings. Besides, we don't have enough gas to go around searching for clothes."

"All right, then. Let's go have a look."

We found five US soldiers lying neatly in a row. They were dressed head to toe in camouflage, and all had a single gunshot wound to the head. Fresh tire tracks had left deep ruts in the grass.

Dr. Trowbridge knelt down to examine the bodies. "It appears they've all been bitten. Some more than once."

"We shot our own guys?" I asked.

"Why not? Considering they had plans to destroy a whole city full of them. Must have left them here during the retreat."

"Ya, but they shot these guys before they turned."

"They are clearly at the mercy of this virus. Wherever they're headed, they didn't want to bring the infection along with them."

Celeste pulled the boots off the shortest of the lot. "This guy is tiny. Look, they're almost my size." She removed his pants and jacket and tried them on.

Dr. Trowbridge and I sized up the fallen soldiers, then removed the uniforms of those closest to us in height.

"His would have fit Alex perfectly," I said, pointing at a skinny corpse.

"He even looks like him," Celeste added. She stared longingly at the fallen soldier.

"Come on friends, we have to keep moving," Trowbridge prodded.

I put my uniform on. It was stained with blood, and it smelled like feces. Celeste did the same.

"I can make this fit," she said, "but it smells like death."

"Mine smells like shit."

"These will have to do," Dr. Trowbridge said. "We can wash them once we find some water."

I took my uniform off, bundled it up, and threw it in the back of the Humvee. "That thing is going to have to wait until it's clean. For now, you two can continue enjoying the Royce show."

Celeste and Dr. Trowbridge followed suit. The three of us jumped in the Humvee and continued bouncing west down the I-70 in our undies.

52.

"Look over there," I said, pointing toward a wooden roadside sign. "Perche Creek one half mile. We can wash our clothes there."

Dr. Trowbridge studied his watch. "That's not a bad idea. We should stay there for the night. Otherwise, we'll get to KC in the dark, and I don't think that's wise, given what we're likely to find."

"Fine with me, doc. What do you say, Celeste?"

"I just hope Perche Creek is cleaner than that river. My hair smells almost as bad as those uniforms."

I turned off the highway and followed the signs to the creek. A short distance down a side road, we came across a drooping one-story building with a tattered tin sign out front that read: Buck's Charge and Chow. Domed polished metal structures stood out front in a tidy row.

"Is this a gas station?" I asked.

"Sort of," Celeste said. "No gas though. It's a charging station."

"Then that's a convenience store. With food!"

"That's doubtful," Dr. Trowbridge explained. "Remember, there's nobody living this close to the front."

"Then why does the sign say 'open'?" I asked, smirking. "I'm gonna have a look."

I parked the Humvee out front, grabbed my rifle, and walked up to the entrance. I placed my hands against the cloudy window and peered inside. There didn't appear to be anyone in there.

Celeste crawled into the driver's seat and stuck her head
out the window. "Hey, Royce, I'll have a BLT, some
Cheetos, and a Diet Coke," she cracked.

"You're gonna eat those words."

I grabbed the front door handle. It was unlocked. I pulled
it open and stepped cautiously inside. The store was layered
with dust and grime. The shelves by the door were stocked
with bubble gum, car air fresheners, sunglasses, and other
items we had no use for. I walked down the aisle and found
a travel box of laundry detergent, which I picked up. I
turned the corner and hit the jackpot. An otherwise barren
snack shelf still had two bags of Doritos and a filthy box of
Twinkies. My eyes grew wide with excitement. I couldn't
wait to prove my companions wrong. I walked over to pick
them up, and was so focused on my achievement that I
missed the shadowy figure emerging from behind the front
counter.

"Afternoon," spoke a raspy voice off to my right.

I spun around and raised my gun almost killing the man
on instinct. I was so shocked to come across a person
instead of a freak that I just stood there. He was an ancient
country bumpkin, complete with flannel shirt underneath
tattered overalls. His greasy white hair competed for
attention with his mangy beard. His eyes were deep set, his
skin leathered from the sun.

"Slow down there, fella. This some kinda stick-up?"

"Oh, no, no, of course not." I lowered my gun. "You can
never be too careful these days."

"Name's Buck. Nice to meet ya. You goin' purchase
that?"

"What, this?" I held the detergent up sheepishly. "Um,
my money is in the car. Just gimme a minute." I put the
detergent on the counter and ran out to the car.

"Empty handed. I knew it!" Celeste said.

I put my hands on the window jam and leaned in. "You two are not going to believe this. There's an old man in there, and he's asking me for money."

"Does he have food?" Celeste asked.

"A little bit, but . . . you just gotta come in and see it for yourselves. I don't think he's all there. It didn't even faze him that I'm in my underwear."

They exited the vehicle and came inside with me. The old man was still standing behind the counter, humming to himself with a vacant expression.

"Hey there, Buck. These are my friends."

My companions looked surprised by the state of the shop. They left footprints in the dust as they approached the counter.

"That'll be fourteen dollars for the soap."

"I'm sorry, sir, but we don't have any money," Dr. Trowbridge said.

"Then you ain't gettin' no soap."

"Of course not," Dr. Trowbridge replied. He studied the old man carefully. "To be perfectly honest, sir, we're surprised to find you here. Last I heard, everyone had been evacuated from this area."

"Evacuated? Don't know nothin' 'bout no evacuation."

"You know, from the war," I said.

"I fought in the war—both of 'em. Freed Kuwait and did two tours in Afghaneestan. We didn't do no evacuatin'."

"Of course you didn't. I wasn't trying to suggest—"

"Did y'all see my pa out there?"

"Who?"

"My pa. He goin' take me to get a new game for my Nintendo soon as he gets home."

"Alrighty, then. Say, Buck, is there a bathroom in this place?" I asked.

"Washroom's out back. This here's the key. Nephew's in there, but don't pay him no mind. Been actin' funny ever since he came back from huntin' so I put him in there till he sobers up."

"Why don't you just go in the woods?" Celeste asked.

"So much better to use the facilities, don't you think?" I asked with an awkward nod toward the door. "Come on you two, it was a long drive. I'm sure you could use some relief."

They followed me outside, and we headed around the building to find the bathroom.

"He clearly has some form of dementia. Most likely Alzheimers," Dr. Trowbridge said.

"You think he's a holdout?" I asked.

"Looks like it. Doesn't seem to mind, given his poor reality testing."

"Poor what?"

"He doesn't know what in the hell is going on."

"Gotcha, doc."

"We can't just leave him here," Celeste said. "He isn't safe. Not anymore."

"We can try. If anyone is willing to hop in a car with a bunch of strangers in their underwear, it's him."

We stopped in front of the bathroom. A ghoul started growling and pawing at the other side of the door as soon as we came near.

"And that would be his nephew," Dr. Trowbridge said. "Here, give me the key. I'm going to open the door."

Dr. Trowbridge unlocked the door and pulled it open. A whisker-faced zombie in shredded camouflage hunting gear came lumbering out of the bathroom toward me. I jammed the bayonet into his eye socket. He fell right to the ground.

"Hey, you just killed his nephew!" Celeste whined.

"What did you think we were going to do with him?"

"I don't know. I just feel bad you know, cause now he's all alone."

"Better alone and in one piece than torn to bits by those you love. That's what I always say. Hey, doc, what should we do with this sack of rocks?"

"Let's just drag him off into the woods," Dr. Trowbridge suggested.

"Like a serial killer," I quipped.

"Yes, Royce, just like a serial killer," Dr. Trowbridge said with a sigh. "Now get over here and help me. The old guy won't even know he's gone."

Dr. Trowbridge and I grabbed the nephew by the ankles and schlepped him back into the trees behind the building. I used the bathroom, and we walked back inside. Our elderly friend was right where we had left him.

"Find er all right?" he asked.

"She's a beauty, Buck. A white porcelain goddess if I've ever seen one. Listen, we're on our way to Kansas City. Gonna check out the sights. How'd you like to come with us?"

"Can't."

"You sure about that? I hear they have a serious selection of Nintendo games and the doctor here is buying."

"Can't leave my store. Got customers to serve."

I took another look at my surroundings as if I might be missing something. "You sure about that, Buck? When was the last time you had a customer?"

"Got customers every day 'cept Mondays. We closed on Mondays. Can't leave my store."

"Should we just grab him?" I asked my friends.

A suddenly lucid Buck overheard my query and pulled a shotgun from behind the counter.

"Ain't nobody gonna be grabbing nobody."

I stepped back and showed my hands. "You're absolutely right, Buck. That was just a silly suggestion."

Dr. Trowbridge stepped forward. "You keep that thing handy, OK? There's a . . . some other folks out there that haven't been acting very neighborly. They're downright rude, actually, and I'm certain they'll be stopping by your establishment from time to time."

"Got no manners, you say?"

"They're extremely angry, and looking for a fight."

"If it's a fight they want, it's a fight they gonna get," the old man growled. He cocked his shotgun.

We walked back out to the Humvee and climbed inside. I tossed a bag of Doritos into Celeste's lap. "They were all out of Cheetos," I said.

"Oh, you didn't!" she squealed.

"What? It's not like he's going to eat them. I got some laundry detergent, too."

We drove down a bumpy dirt road toward the lake, munching on stale Doritos years past their expiration date. They tasted like seasoned cardboard.

"I feel bad leaving him," Celeste said.

"I don't think we had any say in the matter," Dr. Trowbridge pointed out. "We can always check on him tomorrow on our way back out to the highway."

53.

I pulled the Humvee up alongside the creek. We leaned back in our chairs, passing the bag of Doritos around and contemplating our fate. The conversation was lively and focused. It was nice to finally have some down time to process the horror we'd endured.

"Do you really think they can beat this, doc?"

"The vaccination will give them a fighting chance. I don't see how they can overcome this epidemic without it. It's spreading too quickly, and it's impossible to defeat an enemy that's growing exponentially within your ranks. It's going to be a numbers game, even if the immunity works. You have an enemy that doesn't eat, doesn't sleep . . . is always in attack mode. If there's enough of them, and too few of us, all the weapons in the world won't be able to turn the tide."

"What they did to St. Louis. I wonder if that's happening in other cities?" Celeste asked.

"One would have to assume so, at least along the front where there are large concentrations of soldiers. Firebombing St. Louis—that was an act of desperation. It had to have been a last course of action—a dire method to control the number of infected. Let's hope we can get to them in time to even the odds."

"I hope we aren't too late," Celeste added.

"Ya, maybe we should just scrub these things real quick and hit the road. Why are you so worried about getting to KC in the dark?"

"It's a natural point of retreat from St. Louis. I imagine they've reconcentrated their forces there. In the dark, it will be difficult to determine what state the city is in. If the virus has gotten out of control, they'll destroy the city, and we don't want to be in the vicinity when that happens. The fate of our country . . . of humanity . . . may very well depend on our survival."

54.

"Give me some of that detergent," Celeste said. "I'm going to see if it'll wash the stink out of my hair."

"That's not a bad idea," I said.

I poured some of the powder into Celeste's outstretched hands, then grabbed the uniforms and my rifle from the back of the Humvee.

"You coming, doc?"

"No, I'm going to stay here and rest for a moment."

"Suit your stinky self."

Celeste and I walked down the creek a ways to find some privacy. The small, rust-colored body of water, roughly thirty feet across, snaked through a grove of trees. We came across a stretch where the water was less murky.

"I'm going here," she said.

"All right, I'll go find the men's locker room."

The creek careened to the right around a small hill covered in brush. I walked past the hill, set my belongings on the bank, and waded out into the middle of the warm water, which reached my waist. I looked in Celeste's direction to make certain the hill blocked our line of sight. The coast was clear so I slipped off my underwear and returned to the bank. I washed them gently with the soap, wrung them out, and hung them on the bushes to dry.

I dunked the first uniform in the water, sprinkled soap on the areas that looked stained, and rubbed the fabric together as hard as I could. The friction produced a loud scratching sound as it cleaned the soiled fabric. Halfway through the second uniform, I thought I heard something and stopped scrubbing. I looked around for the source of the sound but heard nothing else. I went back to scrubbing. A moment later, I heard something again, and stopped what I was doing. Silence. Then a chilling scream from the other side of the hill.

"Royce!" Celeste screamed desperately.

With no time to waste, I dropped the uniform and ran up and over the hill. I didn't even realize I was naked, nor did I think to grab my gun. Two zombies in US military uniforms had her cornered in the middle of the creek.

"Hey, hey, you dummies, over here!" I yelled and waved my arms to get their attention, then grabbed a cantaloupe-sized rock at the base of the hill and headed out into the water. They stopped for a moment to look at me but then continued after Celeste, who backpedaled and fell onto her backside in the water. I stormed out into the center of the creek yelling to get their attention, to no avail.

I reached the zombie closest to me before he grabbed Celeste. I held the rock in both hands above my head and smashed it down on the top of his skull. The blow blew open a massive crater in the top of his head. He collapsed into the water. The zombie on the other side of her clutched her shoulders and leaned in to bite her on the face. I held the rock in my right hand, swung it back like a bowling ball, then stepped forward, and unloaded it into the zombie's chin. Teeth flew in all directions, and the zombie fell back into the water. It started to get up. I raised the rock and smashed it down on the zombie's forehead. The creature dropped in the water like a stone.

Celeste sloshed over to me, wrapped her arms around my neck, and collapsed sobbing against my chest. I'd never seen her so fragile and vulnerable. She was also nude, and I could feel her firm breasts against my ribs. I rubbed her shoulder and ran my other hand through her hair. Blood from the ghouls clouded the water around us.

"There, there . . ." I whispered softly, "everything's all right. They're gone now."

She cried for a while, then pulled herself together, and asked in a raspy voice, "What happened to your gun?"

"Oh that. It's up on the riverbank. I, um, I heard you scream so I ran right over. I didn't want to leave you alone for another second."

She lifted her head and looked into me like I'd just melted her heart. She grabbed my hand and slid it down her back. She cupped it on her ass and pushed her pelvis up against me. The whole thing took me by surprise. She felt so warm and soft that I was deeply aroused, pulsating against her body.

"Celeste, I have to—"

She placed her finger against my lips then pulled it away and went in for a kiss. Our lips touched for a brief and intoxicating moment. Then I turned my head gently to the side.

"Just wait, I need you to know something. As far as I know, I still have a wife back in California." Celeste's expression morphed into hurt and confusion. "If she's still alive, she's probably a little shriveled old lady, but she's my shriveled old lady. I gave a vow, 'till death do us part.' I want to honor that."

Celeste didn't say a word. Her arms dropped to her sides, and she looked down at the water. She still wore a wounded expression, but something told me she respected my predicament. I didn't know what else to say. The silence and our nakedness were beginning to feel painfully awkward.

Gunfire exploded in the distance. Then silence, followed by another ear-ringing flurry.

"Dr. Trowbridge," I said. "Let me get my gun."

I stomped through the shallow water then stumbled my way up over the sandy hill. I scurried up the bank and grabbed my gun, then returned covered in dirt like a chicken breast dusted with flour. Celeste had put her wet skivvies on and was running with her weapon toward the gunfire. I took off behind her.

There were dead zombies on both sides of the Humvee, all American soldiers, all of them shot in the head. Blood was splattered across the back door. We readied our weapons and walked up to the vehicle. Dr. Trowbridge, covered in blood, lay in his seat. He clutched the base of his neck with both hands. Blood surged between his fingers with every beat of his heart.

"Doc, doc, what do we do? What do we do?" I begged.

"Nothing," he gasped. "Too late for me. Severed my carotid . . . I'm bleeding out."

"What happened?" Celeste asked.

"Fell aslee—"

He stopped speaking and stared blankly off into the distance. The blood stopped flowing through his wound.

"He's gone," I said calmly. Then a flood of emotion rushed over me. "Fucking hell, doc! What are we going to do without you?" I felt like crying. I was naked, tired, and emotionally drained. Another friend had died a horrible death, and the genius behind the cure was no longer there to guide us.

"We have to get out of here," Celeste said. "We have to keep moving."

"You're right. We're better off in the city at night than we are staying here. Who knows how many more of them are out there? We'll just get overrun. Let me go get the clothes."

"OK," Celeste said. "Hurry back."

I started toward the creek but then thought better of it. "You know what? Let's just take the Humvee. Safer that way. I can drive right into the water."

55.

We left the creek and drove back toward the highway. The flame-orange sun was sinking beneath the horizon. The sopping-wet army uniforms we wore were abrasive and cold against the skin, but they preserved our modesty and protected us from lingering thoughts of indiscretion at the center of the creek.

"We have to get Buck," Celeste said. "He won't be safe here anymore."

As difficult, and potentially dangerous, as I knew it would be to bring the deranged old man along with us, doing so was a simple act of humanity. After having unceremoniously left Dr. Trowbridge's body lying in the dirt, as we had with Alex before him, we needed to know we were still human.

I parked the Humvee in front of the Charge and Chow. "Keep watch out here. Just holler if you need me. I'll do the same."

I grabbed my rifle and approached the building. The front door was ajar, held open by a cowboy boot pointing at the sky. A red-faced turkey vulture emerged from the doorway and hopped down the front step as I approached. I waved my gun, and the massive black bird flew over and landed on a rusted out car sitting at the edge of Buck's lot.

I opened the door and saw what had to be Buck, judging by the scraps of bloodied overalls spread around the corpse. The majority of the flesh had been plucked clean from his frame, and the crimson skeleton that remained looked much smaller than the man. I stepped inside the building and slipped on the blood pooled on the floor. I peeked at each side of the aisles. The place looked empty. I grabbed the box of Twinkies and some rose-scented air freshener.

"See any freaks out here?" I asked, climbing back into the Humvee.

"A couple through the binoculars over toward the highway, but other than that, the coast was clear. Where's Buck?"

"See that boot in the doorway?"

"Where?"

"Over there. The one sticking out the door."

"Oh, nooo. Poor old man."

"Ya, it's a real shame. Wish we could've helped him."

We drove down the dirt road and climbed the embankment back on to the highway. Zombies in military uniforms dotted the lanes. Most wandered west toward Kansas City.

"Looks like they're catching up to us," Celeste commented.

"I know. I wonder what it is about the road that draws them. Maybe they like walking on pavement."

"Or maybe their brains know that roads are for traveling."

"Too bad for them their brains don't know that doorknobs are for turning." Celeste smiled at the joke.

"Say, how's your uniform smell?" I asked.

"Better, but still not good." She held her jacket to her nose and sniffed it. "Actually, it's still pretty bad."

"Here, stick this in your pocket." I handed her the rose-scented car air freshener. It was shaped like a pine tree. "A lady like you should smell like a rose."

Celeste tore into the package like it was a Christmas gift. She unbuttoned her front pocket and slid the air freshener inside.

"There," she said. "Good as new. Now pass me a Twinkie."

56.

We motored down the highway toward Kansas City. The closer we got to KC, the more we saw American civilians among the infected. The crowds grew with each passing mile. With the Humvee we could drive over and even through the walking dead.

"Man, look at all of them. I bet they're from the city," I said. "I really hope this doesn't mean it's overrun."

"Me, too. If it is, we better find another route before the bombing starts."

57.

We reached the city limits around midnight. Lights illuminated the windowed skyscrapers dotting the distant skyline.

"Look at that! That's a good sign, huh?" I asked.

"Amazing. There have to be people in there. Real live people."

"I wonder where the army is?"

"Once we find somebody, they can show us the way."

Three cars sped past us from the other direction. I flashed my headlights at them, but they didn't even slow down.

"They're really moving. Too bad they're headed in the wrong direction," I said. "Maybe they can tell us what's going on. Should I go after them?"

"I don't think we should. I doubt they'll stop for us."

I drove further down the highway, weaving through an increasing logjam of wandering ghouls and abandoned vehicles. We pulled up to an ugly scene. A minivan was turned sideways, having crashed into the center divider. The doors were open, and the occupants who had fled were sprawled across the other lanes. A massive zombie mob surrounded them. A thousand or more ghouls—we couldn't see the end of them—clogged the highway, driven to a frenzy by the fresh kill. They were packed in tightly, pressing against and climbing over each other in a quest to tear at the people's flesh.

"Too many cooks in the kitchen," I said.

"That isn't funny. Those poor people. Why do you have to try and make a joke out of everything?"

"I dunno, look at it! It's just . . . it's surreal. Humor is the ultimate chaser. It makes the nastiness a lot easier to swallow."

Celeste still wasn't thrilled with my comment, but at least she knew where I was coming from.

"You think we can drive through there?" she asked.

"Ya, I'm pretty sure this bad boy can drive over anything. I'm going to give it some extra gas to make sure."

"Maybe we should go back and take the side streets?"

"That last exit was four miles ago." I looked at the fuel gauge, which was pegged on empty. Concrete barriers lined the edge of the highway. Even the Humvee couldn't drive over them. We'd have to go all the way back to avoid the mob in front of us. "I don't think we have enough gas to risk it. We gotta go for it."

I backed the Humvee up a ways, shifted into drive, and slammed my foot on the gas pedal. The engine roared to life, and we were moving at a good clip by the time we hit the edge of the zombie horde. The sound of their bodies bouncing off the vehicle started as a machine-gun like progression of thuds, but as we traveled further forward, there were so many of them that the sound—and the sensation—was like we'd landed in a puddle of molasses. Blood and body parts coated the windshield so densely that we couldn't see a thing, but we could feel what was happening and it wasn't good. We started slowing down. I pushed the gas pedal harder, but it was already all the way to the floor. Soon, we weren't moving at all, and our wheels were spinning in place.

"What the hell is going on?" Celeste yelled.

"I don't know! I don't know! I think there are too many of them."

Our tires spun with a dim hiss as they tore through mounds of flesh before sinking down on the pavement in a loud squeal. We still weren't moving forward. Countless hands danced across the bloody windshield. Without any more debris accumulating against the glass, we began to see what we were up against. The highway looked like a Japanese subway car in rush hour. Not a square inch of pavement lay bare. A sea of zombies surrounded the Humvee, beating against the windows. The bulletproof glass was our saving grace.

"Holy shit, Celeste. There's so many of them that we can't move forward."

She grabbed her weapon and cocked it. The Humvee started inching slowly backward.

"You want us to go back? All right, fuckers, let's go back!"

I shifted hard into reverse and the Humvee lurched backward, but the force of the zombies pushing against the vehicle sent it careening back into the center divider. The mob flooded in to fill the gap as I shifted into drive. The vehicle couldn't turn against the rising tide of ghouls. We slammed head-on into the concrete barrier at the edge of the highway.

"Are you all right?" I asked.

"I'm fine, I'm fine," Celeste replied. She looked a little shaken up.

The Humvee slid and rocked from side to side as crowds on both sides pushed against it. The armored doors bulged slightly from the pressure. I shifted into reverse and hit the gas, but it wouldn't move. The sound of untold numbers of ghouls beating on the outside of the vehicle was deafening. It felt like we were trapped inside a tin can.

"What are we going to do, Royce?"

"We're gonna get out of here before they find a way in."
I reached into the back seat and grabbed the remaining
clips of ammunition. I reloaded my gun, tossed one to
Celeste, and shoved the rest into my pockets.

"Put that fresh clip into your gun. You're gonna need as
many rounds as you can squeeze off at once."

"Where are we going to go?"

"We're gonna run for it."

Celeste looked mortified. "We'll never make it, Royce.
There's too many of them out there."

"No, we can. Look . . . the grill is up against that barrier,
right?" She nodded. "There's no one in front of us. We just
need to climb out the ringmount, unload on the freaks
around the hood, and run for it down that embankment.
They aren't fast. If we can break free of them here, I'm sure
we can find a safer place to hide."

"Or better yet, another car."

"That's my girl. Let's do this. You ready? Okay, I'll go up
first, and I'll clear some room for ya. Then you follow."

58.

I popped the hatch on the ringmount and stood from the waist up outside the roof of the vehicle. My presence there up high for all the undead to see caused true hysteria among them. Their groans and screams reached a fevered pitch I hadn't heard since New York. Coarse, veiny hands started grabbing at me from all sides. I fired off single rounds into the heads of those close enough to get ahold of me. I pulled myself up out of the vehicle, balancing precariously on the middle of the roof.

"Celeste, come on up!"

I used the bayonet and bullets to keep our attackers at bay. The roof of the Humvee was wide enough that only the tallest zombies and those standing on top of a fallen ghoul were able to get within grabbing range. The hood was a different story. Since it was much lower to the ground, a sea of arms waited for us to come near.

"Okay, I'm going to work the left side, and you take the right. Just spray the ones standing along the edge. As soon as they go down—run for it. Don't give the ones behind a chance to make their way up to the hood. Leave yourself a few extra rounds if you can."

As usual, Celeste was armed and ready. "Count of three?" she asked. I nodded. "One, two . . . three!"

I started working on my side, careful to get head shots without spraying too many bullets. Celeste meanwhile charged down the windshield and across the hood of the vehicle like a ruthless mercenary, leading with a stream of gunfire that dropped each zombie in her path a split second before she was within reach. She was heading safely down the embankment, and I was still standing on the roof of the Humvee.

My boot slipped in a puddle of blood as I lurched forward to follow Celeste, and my leg slid back right into the grasp of a female ghoul's outstretched arm. I spun around and stabbed my bayonet into the side of her head, then scrambled to my feet as others nearby struggled to get ahold of me. Multiple hands grabbed my pant leg. I pulled forward with all my might. When I broke free, the momentum sent me somersaulting down the windshield and across the hood. I landed with one leg over the concrete barrier and the other wedged between it and the vehicle. My crotch was in the middle of this mess, and when I landed the top of the divider went right into my testicles. What normally would send me rolling on the ground was an afterthought; my body was so flooded with adrenaline. I managed to hold on to my weapon during the fall, and I unloaded my remaining rounds into the gruesome faces of the ghouls that reached in to make a meal of me. I pulled my leg free and spun backwards over the wall onto the grass.

Celeste was at the bottom of the embankment, making her way back to me. I waved her off and lumbered down the embankment, feeling as if someone was squeezing my testicles and my abdomen from the inside. Since I wasn't moving very quickly, I stopped at the bottom of the embankment and looked up the hill to make sure there was enough room between the zombies and me. The mindless ghouls were walking straight into the barrier. It was short enough and they were clumsy enough that they were falling over the barrier by the dozens. They knew what they were after, and as soon as they got on their feet, they stumbled down the hill toward me.

59.

Celeste was waiting for me at the bottom of the hill. We ran toward a strip mall between the highway and a sprawling suburb. The parking lot was lit up like the place was open for business, but only a few cars occupied spaces. The buildings looked empty.

"We better get in one of these cars, quick," I said. "They'll be here soon."

The first car we approached was a four-door family sedan that looked sleek and aerodynamic. It reminded me of the odd concept cars I used to see in auto magazines that would never get produced.

"No keys," Celeste said, peering in the driver's-side window.

"Let's try that one over there."

The next car was a sporty little two seater with clunky, over-sized rims.

"I'd love to meet the douchebag that drives this one," I quipped.

"No keys!" Celeste yelled from the other side of the car.

"Let's make sure this time."

I rammed the butt of my gun into the passenger window. The glass shattered. An ear-piercing alarm started screeching. I opened the door and searched frantically through the glove box, center console, behind the visors, and under the seats. No keys.

"Hurry, Royce, they're getting close."

The zombies were in the parking lot, lumbering toward us. We ran over to a minivan. No keys in the ignition. I reared my weapon back.

"Don't, Royce!"

"Why not?"

"Look behind you."

A fresh crowd of zombies walked out of the neighborhood and into the parking lot. Large groups of the filthy monsters burst forth between the boxy houses like pus squeezing out of a pimple.

"Fuck, fuck fuck! They must be drawn by the alarm. We need to get somewhere safe."

I spun around and scanned my surroundings. The buildings in the strip mall looked like our only options, as droves of undead were encroaching on the perimeter of the parking lot. We ran up to a large sporting goods store and yanked on the door handles.

"It's all barred up in there," Celeste said. "We'll never get through that."

We ran next door to a nail salon. The doors were locked and the windows free of bars.

"Not this one, not this one. We can't barricade ourselves in there once we break the glass," I said.

I turned and looked to my right, toward the highway. A McDonald's sat at the edge of the parking lot. The lights were on inside, and I could see someone watching us through the window.

"Celeste, you see that? See that guy in there? Let's go."

We sprinted to the McDonald's weaving between the zombies in the parking lot. When the gaps were too tight to run through, I put my shoulder down like a football player and knocked them to the pavement. It was risky business, but we were out of options. There weren't enough of the oafish ghouls to get hold of us.

When we reached the McDonald's, we pounded on the front door. There was someone inside—a pimple-faced teenager with curly, platinum blond hair. He was dressed in a wrinkled McDonald's uniform with navy slacks, a powder blue shirt, and a red tie. His cap had a big yellow M stitched into the front. We stood there anxiously as he made his way over to the doorway. He looked skeptical, but he moved to unlock the door. Then he stopped and pointed behind us.

We turned and looked. Zombies coming from the highway had redirected to the building. The fastest ones were closing in on us. They had fewer wounds and looked fresher than the others, at least in death, and they walked at a pretty good clip.

"I need to reload," I said, digging a clip out of one of my deep uniform pockets. "I'm grabbing a freshie for you, too."

Celeste was methodic in firing her weapon. She was a great shot, even from a distance, and she dropped our attackers one at a time with rhythmic strikes to the head. Celeste's weapon clicked. I handed her a clip, then I went to work with my rifle. I was a terrible shot from long range. I was only able to pop off a bunch of shoulder shots, whiffs over the head, and a partial removal of one ghoul's ear. This wasn't slowing their progress, so I squeezed the trigger and held it down, unleashing a spray of bullets that felled three zombies before my weapon clicked.

Celeste had reloaded by this time, and she was dropping attackers from all directions in rapid succession. In between shots, we heard the key turn in the lock behind us with a click. The boy opened the door, and we backed inside. He slammed the door shut and locked it. The zombies outside began pounding on the glass.

"Come in the back," he said. "I had a few do this before, and they left after a while once they couldn't see me."

"They'll break their way through the glass before they'll go away," I said. "I've seen 'em do it."

"This should help," he said. The boy walked behind the counter and pushed a button behind the cash register. Metal bars slid down from a compartment in the ceiling and covered the windows. They looked like the kind of metal grate you'd expect to find protecting a pawnshop in the seedy part of town.

"You need those to keep people from breaking into a friggin' McDonald's?"

The boy was confused by my question.

"There's a lot more crime now," Celeste whispered to me. She smiled nervously at the boy like I was some kind of mental patient.

We walked into the back and sat down on the floor against a dormant fryer. The front counter shielded us from the zombie's view.

"You two in the army or something?" the boy asked.

"No, no, we came from New York," I said.

"New York? Really? How'd you make it all the way here?"

"The Chinese military is pretty much trashed, son."

"I'm Jason."

"Oh, sorry, Jason. I'm Royce, and this is Celeste. Ya, they've pretty much all turned into these freaks. We just had to stay out of their claws to make it this far."

"What are you doing at work with all of those things out there?" Celeste asked.

"I've been in here since yesterday. I heard rumors during school of people getting sick and some weird stuff happening in the city, but the kids at school are always saying all kinds of crap so I didn't take it seriously. I went home and played video games all afternoon. When it was time for my shift, I went to work. My boss is the biggest dick you'll ever meet, so I knew he'd want us to work no matter what. Everything seemed normal on my way over here, but then no one was inside the building, and some of those kooks came after me in the parking lot. I locked myself in here, and I've been here ever since."

"Did you drive here, Jason?" Celeste asked. "Are one of those cars yours?"

"I don't have a car. I have a moped."

"That's not going to get us out of here, Jace," I said. "Who do you know that has a car?"

"My parents, my friends . . . lots of people. But the phones aren't working for some reason, and no one has come by. I thought for sure somebody would come to get me by now." Jason looked despondent.

"Don't worry," Celeste said. "I'm sure they're fine. They're holed up somewhere safe and sound just like you are."

Jason took comfort in that.

"So, this is the first you've seen of the freaks, eh Jace?" I asked.

"Yes. What's wrong with them?"

"It's a disease . . . a virus. Makes you go all cuckoo and want to eat people. And you know what the worst of it is?"

"No," he said, shaking his head.

"They're already dead. The virus kills you, and when you come back to life, you're a flesh-eating monster, just like they are." I pointed toward the front door.

Jason gulped audibly.

"Royce, stop it! You're scaring him."

"He should be scared. I'm scared of those things." I turned back to Jason. "I'll tell you the secret, Jace. Don't get bit. Even the littlest nip from one of those freaks is all it takes to catch the disease."

"And there's a cure," Celeste added.

"There is?" Jason asked.

"Yes, there's a vaccine."

"We're the only ones who know what it is," I said. "Celeste and I are both immune. We injected her with the virus, and nothing happened."

"Really?"

"Really."

Jason wasn't convinced. He looked at Celeste who confirmed my suggestion. "Do you have any more?" he asked.

"Nope, but the military does. They're sitting right on top of it and they don't even know it. That's why we're here. We need to find them and tell them about the cure."

"Did they come to Kansas City?" Celeste asked.

"They're always here, on account of how close we are to the front and all, but ya, a whole bunch of them started rolling into town yesterday morning. They started building a bunch of barricades downtown. Said everything was fine, and we should go about our business."

"They still have a lot to learn," Celeste said.

60.

We slept on the stained linoleum behind the counter. The ghouls' constant moaning had become white noise. It was like having an apartment downtown by the train tracks—eventually, you can sleep right through the shaking.

When I woke up in the morning, I peeked over the counter. I couldn't believe my eyes. More zombies than I had ever seen surrounded the building. There were literally thousands. Men carrying briefcases, pregnant women, police officers, toddlers with binkys in their mouths, you name it. One glimpse of me, and they were up against the glass again, pounding and pushing.

"Guys, guys, wake up!" I yelled, crouching down behind the counter. "We have a *big* problem."

I crawled on my hands and knees over to the drive-through window and stood up cautiously to look outside. They were out there in droves just as they'd been out front. From what I could see, the mob stretched all the way around the building. Just as I was about to duck down, I saw a zombie wearing the same uniform as Jason, sans hat. Maybe it was just a coincidence, but he walked right up to the window like he owned the place. His nametag read: Richard, Manager. Imagine that, I thought, the dick's name is Dick.

Celeste and Jason were waking up as I crawled back over to the counter.

"What is it?" she asked.

"Take a look out front. Just don't let them see you."

Celeste stuck her head up from behind the counter. She ducked back down. Her eyes were as wide as saucers. "There's so many of them. It's like the whole city is out there."

They must have seen her surface because the moaning reached a fevered pitch, and we could hear glass breaking in the lobby. We all looked over the counter. The zombies had broken several windows and were smashed up against the bars, which bowed a couple of feet inside the restaurant. It was enough for one of them to slide through the gap at the bottom if they were clever enough to figure that out.

"They're going to come in," Jason cried.

"They won't climb through that gap," I said. "They're too stupid. Might break through those bars though. They'll just smash themselves into them like they did the glass."

"Those bars are pretty strong," Jason said.

"How strong?"

"They're made out of some kind of super-strong material. Somebody tried to drive a truck through the front door a few months ago, and the bars didn't break."

"Let's hope they hold. That's a lot of pressure from all those bodies."

61.

We spent the rest of the morning sitting behind the counter drinking bottled water and eating sundae toppings while we listened to the zombies breaking the glass and flexing the bars.

"We're never gonna make it out of here," I said, tossing a handful of chopped nuts in my mouth. As hopeless as my comment sounded, I believed it to be true. I was never going to see my family again.

"We have to," Celeste said. "We have to spread the cure. There has to be a way out."

"Not through them there isn't. Besides, if we try and don't make it (which we won't), then they'll never know about the cure."

"You're beginning to sound like Alex," she said. I gave her a sour look. I wanted to say something mean but thought better of it given how long they'd been friends.

"What happened to the guy that fought his way in and out of the rations depot?"

"Those weren't suicide missions." I reached into my pocket and pulled out the last three magazines. "This is all the ammo we've got. This one isn't even full. It isn't enough to get through those freaks."

"Well, so is staying here. You see the way things are going out there. You know what's coming next."

"What's coming next?" Jason asked, flipping his tie nervously.

"Nothing, dude, don't worry," I said, giving Celeste the stink eye. "Now you're scaring him." I tried to change the subject. "Say, Jason, what happened to your name tag?"

"My name tag? I dunno . . . I never put it on since I'm not working. Why?"

"Cause I found your boss, that's why."

"Really? Where is he?"

"Outside the drive-through window. His name is Rich, right?"

"Ya, it's Rich. Is he one of those things?"

"You got it, buster. Wanna shoot him?"

"Royce!" Celeste barked.

"What? He's already dead. You can put him out of his misery and live out a fantasy at the same time. How many people get to waste their boss and don't have to spend the rest of their life in prison?"

Jason looked interested but afraid to speak. I retrieved my weapon from next to the cash register. "You want to fire this bad boy, don't ya?"

He nodded.

"You know this thing has a laser on it? Mine's broken (long story), but it comes out when you press this button right here. Thing is freaking awesome."

"Jason, you're going to have to pass for now," Celeste said. "We don't want to rile those things up any more than they already are."

"Awww, Mom, you're always ruining all the fun," I said. "Actually, she's right. That's probably a bad idea—for now. We'll find a good time for you to let him know what you really think of this job."

62.

It was another excruciatingly boring day in hiding. I hated the inactivity coupled with the anxiety of being cornered by thousands of creatures that wanted nothing more than to eat us. The zombies out front sniffed incessantly, so we moved further back into the restaurant so they couldn't smell us. We sat between the grill and the freezer.

"If they break through the gates, we should go in the freezer," Celeste said. "They'll never be able to open the handle."

"That's a good idea," I said, yawning. I noticed a sign next to the heat lamps that had instructions for giving a McRib "fresh off the grill flavor."

"You guys still have the McRib!"

"What do you mean *still*? We have it every year," Jason said.

"Can you make me one?"

"Oh gross," Celeste moaned. "You like those things?"

"Like them? I love them."

"Did you know they have a flour-bleaching agent in them that's also used to make yoga mats?" she asked.

"Nope, but I'm not surprised, and I don't care. I wouldn't expect anything less from my favorite restructured meat product."

"You know what? I think I can," Jason said. "We cook them over there, so they shouldn't be able to see me, except when I get the pickles."

"I gotta have the pickles. Don't worry about grabbing them. Those freaks already know we're in here. Just do it fast so they don't get too worked up."

Jason went into the freezer, retrieved some frozen "rib" patties, and started making me a sandwich.

"Sure you don't want one, Celeste?" I asked.

"I'll stick to the nuts."

In true fast food fashion, Jason was back with the piping hot sandwich in a matter of minutes. I was savoring my second bite of the delicate, tangy goodness when I heard a familiar rumbling sound outside. I dropped my sandwich and ran out into the center of the restaurant. Three Humvees and an armored personnel carrier came storming into the parking lot. A fifty-caliber machine gun was mounted on each vehicle. Gunners stood behind the weapons, poised and ready for a fight.

"We're in here! We're in here!" I yelled, jumping up and down and waving my arms above my head.

The vehicles approached the McDonald's and stopped about thirty feet from the edge of the zombie horde. Each gunner hurled multiple neutron grenades into the heart of the crowd and opened fire on the zombies as they ran toward the vehicles. The fifty-caliber bullets tore through the ghouls and the walls of the building without slowing down. I turned to Celeste and Jason, who had come out from behind the counter.

"Get down!" I yelled.

They dove behind the counter, and I was hoping to join them when a bullet struck me in the back. Time seemed to slow down after the bullet passed through me. It shattered the cash register and left a massive crater in the door of the metal freezer. I fell to my knees. I looked down at the wound. It looked like a tin can had traveled through me. I fell on my left side and started coughing up blood. Celeste crawled out from behind the counter. She screamed my name and held my face. I blacked out.

63.

I woke up in a small room with a low ceiling. That's all I could see anyway. There were machines on either side of me. I was lying on my back, and it hurt too much to turn on my side. My upper body had a deep ache. The space hummed loudly, and vibrated slightly. Sometimes, I wasn't sure if it was me or the room that was shaking.

"There he is," a voice announced. "Mr. Nine Lives is back again." A tall barrel-chested soldier stood beside me. He wore the same camouflage uniform we'd stolen, and he looked like GI Joe, wide-jawed and smiling.

"Why are you calling me that?" I coughed. The pain in my chest was excruciating.

"Your friends told us all about you. Frozen and brought back to life forty years later—that's incredible. You died in the year I was born, you know that?"

I didn't say anything.

"That's all right, save your energy, hoss. My name's Neal. I'm going to be keeping an eye on you for a while."

I held out my hand. Neal shook it gently.

"We thought we might lose you there for a moment. Most people don't survive a direct hit with a fifty-cal round."

"There's a cure," I whispered. "Smallpox . . ."

"Save your breath, now. Your friend, Celeste, she told us all about it. They ran some tests back in Alameda, and by God, the damn thing works! We got lucky on this one. The government stockpiles the smallpox vaccine. They're going to immunize everybody. It's going to take some time, but they're working on it as we speak."

"Where's Celeste?"

"She left for Montana a couple days ago. They found some of her family there."

"And Jason?"

"He's fine, too. The boys rescued you all once they realized you were in that McDonald's. Sergeant Jenkins feels terrible for shooting you. It's hard to see the friendlies when there's that many bodies moving around. Anyway, Jason went with the rest of the evacuees to a camp outside Wichita. We lost Kansas City. Had to put her down like St. Louis and Minneapolis. Jackson, too, now, as of yesterday."

"How did all this happen so fast?"

"You've been in a coma for the last four days. Docs induced it. Reduces the stress on the body from all the surgeries. They pulled you out of it this morning and cleared you to go home. Been sleeping ever since."

"Where am I?"

"On a flight to San Diego."

"I am?" The sudden rush of excitement threw me into a coughing fit.

"That's where you're from, right?"

I nodded.

"My wife . . . my son." I choked.

"We'll try to look them up when we land. Your last name is Bruyere, correct? We didn't know their names so we figured we'd wait for you to come to so you can help us. San Diego is a pretty big place these days, given its distance from the front. We didn't want to contact every Bruyere in the county and tell them a frozen relative came back from the dead to see them. Know what I mean?"

I nodded, but my mind was already in another place. I couldn't believe I was on my way home. I wondered if my family was still alive and the journey had been worth it. I was so close to realizing my dream that I pushed the doubt out of my mind. I refused to tolerate the thought of living without them.

"Get some rest," he said, patting me on the belly.

I winced in pain.

"Oh, sorry, hoss. We land in an hour. I'll fetch you some painkillers so you can be up and at 'em."

64.

I almost refused the painkillers. I hated the groggy feeling I got from Vicodin, but these things were incredible. Neal gave me two tablets as the jet approached San Diego. After we landed, he fetched me. It had hurt so much to move that I was hesitant to try to sit up. Neal finally grabbed me by the shoulders and lifted me into a seated position. I cringed the whole way up and then realized the pain I was feeling was psychological.

"Go ahead, stand up," he said.

I got to my feet and rotated my torso. I didn't feel even the slightest tinge of pain.

"What on earth did you give me? This stuff is unreal!"

"First time on Renidol, I take it?"

"First time for everything lately."

"The best part about it is you won't get addicted to it. Just take a tablet every eight hours until the soreness from your surgeries subsides."

The jet had a side door just like a passenger jet, and we walked down a set of portable steel stairs to the tarmac.

"Is this Miramar?" I asked.

"You still recognize it, eh?"

"I lived in San Diego my whole life. You guys didn't really change the base all that much."

"Good point. Come this way."

We walked past an enormous hangar and two neat rows of midnight black, Stealth helicopters parked out front. Long one-story buildings with few windows ran alongside the hangar. They reminded me of barracks. We entered the third one, and I was surprised to see the bustling office inside. The space was divided into cubicles. Men and women in uniform were in meetings, on telephones, and working with computers similar to the one we saw in Weston.

"Man, everything here is just so . . . normal, I guess. I've seen some really weird shit since I left New York."

"You might be seeing more of it, hoss. That virus is spreading pretty quickly. Let's hope they can administer your cure fast enough."

"It's not my cure. Dr. Andrew Trowbridge is the one who discovered it. We lost him outside St. Louis. He was a very brave man."

"Yes, I've been informed."

We walked down the corridor between cubes, and everyone we passed stared at us. Some whispered to each other, others saluted, but everyone stopped what they were doing.

"They're saluting you, too, you know."

"Why me?"

"You're a hero."

"A hero? What did I do?"

"You brought us the cure, and through hostile enemy territory at that."

"Not even. I'm just a guy that didn't get sick because of dumb luck. My friends who didn't make it—they're the real heroes. I wouldn't be here without them."

"A lot of people are saying that you and Celeste have saved us. If all our forces weren't busy fighting those things and rolling out the cure, there'd be a lot of pomp and circumstance to your homecoming."

"Like you said, the virus is still spreading. All we did was try and save ourselves."

65.

Neal took me to a cubicle, and we sat in front of a computer. He brought up a list of women in San Diego with the last name Bruyere. My wife was not among them. My heart sank.

"How about the rest of the country? Can you show me that?"

She wasn't on that list either. I felt sick to my stomach.

"Maybe she changed her name," Neal suggested.

"Why would she do that?"

"Uh, you died forty years ago. She probably remarried."

I felt like such a fool. I hadn't even considered the possibility that she'd remarried. Rationally I knew that forty years had passed, but in my heart, in my thoughts, she was the same woman I kissed goodbye on the day I died.

"My son . . . his name is Colt. Please look him up."

He spun alphabetically through a new list of names. As soon as he came upon Bruyere, I spotted Colt's name in the middle of the mix. I leapt up from my chair and tried to point to Colt's name on the projected image. My finger went right through it.

"That's him, that's my son! Right there, Colt Bruyere."

"Eight Zero Two North Rios Avenue. You know where that is?"

"Of course," I said. "I knew he'd stay in the neighborhood," I muttered to myself.

"Would you like to call him?"

"Yes, yes, I mean no. I don't know. Should I call him?"

"I would, but that's your call, hoss."

"I would, it's just . . . it's so weird, that's all. What if he doesn't believe me?"

Neal shrugged. "You've been all over the news."

"Even weirder."

"We can take you there, if you'd like."

"Good idea. It'll be so much better face to face. Let's go see if he's home."

66.

Neal drove me off the base in a white, solar van with government plates. My hometown had changed so much I hardly recognized it. The buildings were taller and densely packed. Areas that had once been quiet suburbs looked like mini-cities. The traffic was terrible on freeways that crisscrossed in every direction. It looked more like Los Angeles than San Diego. It took us forty-five minutes to get up to Colt's house on the coast, but it felt like hours. I was so excited to see him, but apprehensive at the same time. I felt guilty for crashing the plane. He knew better than anyone that I shouldn't have been flying that day. I grieved for his mother. I couldn't bear the fact that I'd never see my beautiful wife again.

We pulled up in front of the address from the computer and parked against the curb. I remembered the house vividly. It was the quintessential Southern California stucco track home, one of just a few built on the street. It was completed in the late nineties and hadn't been remodeled. It still felt like a new home to me, even though it had become a cozy, aging relic among a neighborhood of angular, glass-covered marvels.

"I'll stay out here until you're done," Neal said.

"Actually, I could use a little space."

"And if he isn't home?"

"That's okay. I'll just go for a walk, check out the neighborhood, and stuff."

"I'll come back to check on you at sixteen hundred hours. Here's my number if you need to reach me before then. We can provide a place to stay if you need." He handed me a plain white business card with the Marine Corps globe and anchor printed prominently on the front.

"Thanks."

I got out of the car and walked slowly toward the front door. Neal gave me a quick nod as he took off down the street. It felt like Dad had just dropped me off for my first day of school, I was so anxious. I pushed the doorbell, and the chime echoed inside the house. The door opened, and I recognized Colt immediately. My boy was no longer a young man. He was older than me. My heart opened wide, but my timid mouth remained shut.

"It's you! It's really you!" he screamed. He grabbed me in a tight hug.

I hugged him back as hard as I could, bawling. The joy of seeing him again was greater than any I'd experienced. We remained there for a moment, locked in the embrace.

"Let me get a look at you," I said, pulling my head back and putting my hands on his face. "You're an old man now like your father. Imagine that."

"You look just like I remember, Dad. You're like a walking photograph. I can't believe you're really here." He gave me another hug.

"How did you know I was coming?"

"It was all over the news. They kept saying your name and how you'd been frozen in twenty ten and brought back to life in New York. The first time I heard that I just about fell out of my chair. I didn't know what to believe. There's been so much misinformation since the war started. It all sounded too good to be true."

"Now you believe it?"

"Of course. They're also saying you're a hero. That you're a gift from the past who found the vaccine and brought it across the front."

"That's the part you shouldn't believe."

"Then how'd you get here?"

"There'll be time for that. I want to talk about you. You stayed in the neighborhood, eh?"

"I did. I love it here. I also wanted to be close to Mom. Here, come inside."

We walked into the house. It was smartly decorated and cozy inside. It definitely had a woman's touch. We went into the living room and sat on the couch. There was a picture on the mantle of Colt frolicking in the grass with a petite blonde woman and two angelic little towheaded girls.

"What a beautiful family!"

"I'm a lucky man."

"That you are. At least until they're teenagers."

"I can't say I'm looking forward to that. This is Molly and that's Linea."

"How old are they?"

"Molly is nine now, and Linea is seven."

"Wow, you two waited a long time to have kids."

"They're our little war babies. Actually, a lot of people wait until their mid-forties to have kids now, so we weren't too late. Candice and I were so focused on our careers that the years just flew by. Then the war started, and our perspective changed. We got pregnant right away. She's a little younger than me, so that helped."

"When can I meet them?"

"Tonight. They'll be home around six. We should have dinner."

"That'd be marvelous, son. Say, you look a little pale. I take it you haven't been in the water lately?"

"I'm afraid not. Only a couple of times since the war started. It's really frowned upon."

"Frowned upon?"

"Ever since we've had the Chinese on our front porch. You have to understand, Dad. It's a different world now. Most every waking hour of every single day is spent defending our country. It's been a real struggle to keep this half of America free. I miss surfing a lot, but I have to defend my family's freedom."

"So you're a soldier?"

"No, I'm an engineer, but like most people, I dedicate my craft to the cause. Which reminds me, I might need to take a phone call at some point. I work from home, and I've been fielding a lot of urgent requests today."

"Are you serious? You haven't seen me for forty years, and you're going to work?"

"The shift from fighting the Chinese to fighting this disease hasn't been easy. We have a lot of work to do if we're going to contain it."

I was proud of his dedication. Still, I felt dejected, but I tried to hide it.

"Dad, you were right in the middle of this outbreak, weren't you?"

"Ya, I've seen some things."

"I can't allow it to come here. I've heard some horrible things. My little girls can't see that."

"Of course. Don't worry about me. I'll just, um—listen, before you go anywhere, I have something I want to tell you."

"Sure, Pop."

"You can't imagine how sorry I am for leaving you and Mom like I did. I should have been there for you two. All those years . . . I should have been right here."

"I'm not going to lie to you, Pop. It was hard. It was really hard on us for a very long time, but eventually we started to enjoy life again. Not as much as if you were with us, but we knew you'd want us to carry on."

"There are so many things we didn't get to share. I should've been there when my little granddaughters were born, when you graduated, and the surfs. Oh the surfs! I waited forever for you to get big enough to surf with me, to travel with me, and what happened to that? I threw most of our best years together right in the garbage."

Colt's eyes grew swollen and moist. I moved next to him and put my arm around him.

"I just want you to know that I'm sorry. That I realize what I've done. I wish I could take it all back."

I noticed Colt's right hand resting on his leg. The ring and pinky fingers were missing.

"What happened to your hand?"

"I lost them in the plane crash. The doctors couldn't reattach them. They were too mangled."

"I never should have flown that plane."

"Maybe so, but who really knows? What if we'd landed safely, or you didn't have that heart attack? The plane isn't what killed you."

"It's still my fault."

"You're missing the point. It doesn't matter whose fault it is. That was almost forty years ago. Sure, it was a slow, painful process for us in the beginning, but we've had a long time to heal."

"I wish I could accept that."

"The whole thing must be really fresh for you."

"It sure is."

"It isn't for us, Pop. We lost you so long ago. Sure, I wish I could have spent those years with you. There are so many things I would have loved to share, but that's the past. Those years are gone. None of that matters now because you're back. You're right here with me, and that's an incredible gift. It's a miracle."

"I guess it'll take some time for me to come to terms with my regret. It hasn't even been two weeks since they thawed me out. It's so great seeing you, son. I didn't know if I was going to make it out here alive, but now that I did—now that I'm sitting here in your living room—I realize everything I've missed."

"You're going to have to learn how to take the good with the bad. If there's one thing I've learned from the last ten years, it's that."

"I guess you're right. If you had been living back east, I never would have found you."

"That's the spirit, Pop. And you—you were crazy enough to fly that plane, but you were also crazy enough to get frozen. That's the only reason you're here now. How many people get that second chance?"

"Um, nobody. I'm the only one."

"Exactly. We're going to embrace this opportunity for what it is. We'll just have to make up for the time we lost."

"I never thought about it that way. I just wish I could do the same for your mother. Oh God how I let her down. We were supposed to grow old together. All those anniversaries, birthdays . . . sunsets on the porch—they're all gone. I should have been there for her, right by her side, but now it's too late. There's nothing I can do to make up for it."

"So they told you about her."

"Oh, no, no. It's true isn't it?"

"What's true?"

"I'll never get over her. She was the love of my life. Please tell me she went peacefully."

"Went? She didn't go anywhere. She still lives in the house on the cliff."

"You mean she isn't . . . dead?"

"No, of course not."

I leapt up from the couch. "Are you serious? I have to see her. Is she home now?"

"Probably. She's getting older now so she doesn't spend a lot of time outside the house."

"What a relief! I don't know why, I just—when I didn't see her name in the database, I assumed the worst."

"Dad, you didn't see her in the database because her last name isn't Bruyere anymore. She remarried."

"Oh." My heart sank, as did I, back into the couch.

"Don't take it hard. She mourned you for a very, very long time. She was incomplete without you. She lived like half a person. That's literally what everyone said. Eventually, though, life goes on. Even Mom had to move on with her life. She had no other choice."

"Maybe that was my time, that day in the plane. I should have just died when nature intended."

"You don't mean that."

I did mean it, but I bit my tongue. It wasn't right for me to show up after all those years only to upset my son.

"You wouldn't want to deprive Mom of happiness, would you?"

"No, of course not. This is just one of those things that's hard for me to get used to. Half a lifetime has passed for you since the crash, but for me, nothing has changed. It's like it was yesterday . . . I'm still stuck in twenty ten."

"You belong here, Pop. You belong in this world."

"I hope you're right. I really do. Let me ask you a question."

"Shoot."

"Is she happy now?"

"Yes, she is, but she'll be a lot happier once she sees you again."

A phone rang loudly upstairs.

"You need to get that?"

"I probably should. Why don't you go see Mom?"

"Okay, I will."

"I'll head over there as soon as I'm done here."

67.

I didn't know why, but I ran all the way to my house. While I waited for the light to turn so I could cross the Coast Highway, people stared and pointed at me from their vehicles. They must have recognized me from the news. As soon as I caught sight of my home, I lost the urge to run. I stopped and tried to catch my breath. The neighbors had gone bananas—gaudy mansions cluttered the street, depriving it of any character.

Like Colt's dwelling, my house had changed little since I last saw it. It was nice to know that some things had withstood the test of time. I had worked my whole life to buy that house, and now I was afraid of it, apprehensive of what it held inside. I opened the front gate, walked past the front door, and stood on the edge of the deck overlooking the ocean. Groomed lines from a healthy south swell followed the edge of the reef beneath the house. Colt wasn't exaggerating about surfing being taboo. There wasn't a single person in the ocean. Even the lifeguard station was boarded up.

I knocked softly on the door. It was a strange sensation, being an uninvited guest at my own home. An old man answered. He must have been at least eighty years old. I recognized a familiar face buried beneath the wrinkles and liver spots.

"Gary, is that you?"

"Royce! Welcome home! We saw you on the news this morning, and now here you are. Well, aren't you a bolt from the blue."

"So you're the one that's giving it to my wife?"

"Oh Royce, now . . . take it easy, friend."

"Just answer the question. Are you or aren't you?"

"Come on, pal. It's not like you were off on deployment or something. You've been dead for forty years. What did you expect?"

"I expect my friends to keep their hands to themselves."

"Royce, buddy, I'm sorry. We're so excited to have you back. It doesn't have to be like this."

I heard someone stirring in the background. I leaned in closer and spoke softly, "You know what's ironic about all this, Gary? When I first woke up, I thought you were playing a prank on me. The weird clothes, funny-looking machines, the mean Chinese doctors . . . I thought you were sticking it to me. Turns out you really are sticking it, just not to me."

"Look," he said gruffly. "I'm going to step out and give you two some space." He grabbed a pair of shoes from inside the doorway, hobbled over to the bench out front, and pulled them on with his shaky, bony hands. "I really am glad to see you, Royce" he said, patting me on the shoulder as he walked past.

"Royce Bruyere, you come inside," a familiar voice called from inside the house.

I stepped into the entry, and there was my wife, sitting in a chair in the living room just like the last time I saw her. She was tiny. The passing years had robbed her of muscle tone and shrunk her frame. Her wrinkled skin hung loose on her bones. She looked and sounded a lot like her mother, which was shocking, but her spark and infectious smile—immune to the ravages of time—were all her own.

"Oh dear, you're as handsome as the day we first met," she said.

I walked over to her, and she pulled herself up gingerly out of the chair. She placed her lips gently against mine. "I was always afraid of what being frozen was going to do to your face. I just never suspected that it would be any of my concern."

"Here I am," I said awkwardly.

She started sobbing. I held her tight. She felt so little, like a fraction of her former self. My eyes felt heavy, but the tears wouldn't fall.

"I always used to say that I'd trade anything, anything at all, for another day with you . . . " She smiled, her face streaming with tears.

"You and Colt are all I've thought about. There were times when I didn't know if I'd make it here alive, but I kept pressing on. I didn't want to live if I wasn't with you."

"Were you hurt? They say that disease makes people do terrible things."

"Just a little bit from the freaks. There was a doctor, though, and he fixed me up. Then I got shot. By our own troops, if you can believe it," I said, laughing. "Look at this." I opened my shirt to expose the massive scar on my chest. "It happened just a few days ago, and here I am, good as new. I just have to take one of these pills every eight hours." I held up the little bottle and shook it.

"It's shocking what they can do. Do you remember what Restora said when we signed you up for the service? That it would take hundreds, maybe thousands of years before they could bring you back?"

"If they could do it at all. Those Chinese . . . they are something else. I don't know what they did to me, but I feel better than I did before the accident."

"Do you remember everything?"

"Everything. Like it was yesterday."

"Then you must be disappointed by this little old lady you found living in our house."

"Never. The only person I'm disappointed in is myself. I never should have left you alone. I was rash. Impulsive. I threw our life away, for what? I'll never forgive myself for that."

"Royce, you have to forgive yourself. Do you know why?"

"No."

"Because I've forgiven you."

I didn't know what to say. Her intent was a hard thing for me to accept.

"Colt told me why you flew home that night."

"I wanted to make our date."

"You're a sweet, sweet man, and we had a wonderful twenty-five years together. Can't we just let the past be the past?"

"I'm trying. I really am. It's hard for me because it doesn't feel like the past. It feels like everyone changed except for me."

"Is that why you were so mean to Gary?"

"Don't even get me started with him."

"I'm eighty-five years old, Royce. Gary turns ninety in January. We married thirteen years ago, after he lost Donna. It just felt right. We take care of each other. We keep each other company."

I stared at the floor like a hurt little child while she spoke.

"Oh, Royce, it's not like we're a couple of twenty somethings running around christening every room in the house."

"You mean like we did?" I asked with a sheepish grin.

"Of course I do. You gave me the best years of my life. No one can take that away from us."

"I'm sorry, love. You'll have to forgive me for what I said to Gary. It's just that . . . you don't know what I went through to get here. That virus is a horrible thing, and all along I had this image in my head—I was driven by it—an image of you and Colt, of our life together before the accident. I think I secretly wished that nothing had changed. That I'd get here and my life would return to what it was. Now that I see the two of you here in the flesh I know that the world just kept on spinning without me."

"Royce, we're still here. We're your family, and nothing can change that. Just focus on us, don't be distracted by everything else."

"Like another man sleeping in my bed?"

"Yes, like another man sleeping in your bed. You'll have to embrace this world for what it is. There's so much you haven't seen yet. Like the girls, have you seen the girls?"

"Just a picture when I was over at Colt's place."

"They will melt your heart. You're going to adore being a grandparent. It's simply wonderful."

"Hey, that reminds me. Colt invited me to dinner tonight so I could meet the girls. Why don't you and Gary come along?"

"Are you sure?"

"Sure. Like you said, we're family."

68.

We spent the next few hours catching up. The time flew. Age hadn't tarnished her wit and penchant for breakneck conversation. Talking to her in our living room for hours on end reminded me of when we first started dating. We'd stay on the phone late into the night. She got me up to speed on our friends and family—who was still alive, who had died, who got divorced, who came out of the closet, the whole nine yards. It was a lot to take in, but it sure did bring me into the present.

We were interrupted when Colt came barging through the front door.

"Some things never change," I said. "The kid still doesn't knock."

"Are you kidding, Pop? Why would I?"

"Hey, I invited Mom and Gary to dinner tonight. Is that okay with you?"

"Sure, that'll be great. Hey, Mom, you mind if I borrow Dad for a bit?"

"Of course, honey. I should probably give Gary a call and let him know it's safe to come home now."

"Safe? What's that supposed to mean?" Colt asked.

"Nothing," I said. I gave her a sarcastically dirty look and ushered Colt toward the open door. "Where are you taking me?"

"Come on, it's a surprise."

"Ooh, I like surprises," I said, rubbing my hands together in anticipation. We stepped out front and closed the door behind us. "Hey, come check this out." I led Colt onto the deck and pointed at a wave that danced across the reef below. "Look how good it is. And there isn't a soul out!"

"That's the thing, Dad. I got off work early because the freaking commandant himself called me. He said that you and the woman you were with are war heroes."

"War heroes? That's silly. We aren't even soldiers."

"The president himself is going to give you the Presidential Medal of Freedom."

"This whole world is off its rocker." I shook my head. "I guess if it gets you off work it can't be all bad."

"Ya, that's the thing. The commandant told me I've been reassigned. He says my new job is to make sure you get acclimated and get plenty of R&R. He said nothing is off limits. We can do whatever you want."

"Cool, where's the nearest strip club?"

"Hardy, har. Just stay here for a second, okay?"

I stayed on the deck, mesmerized by the waves. I don't know how long Colt was gone, but he returned with a surfboard under each arm. Towels and wetsuits were draped across them. I recognized the board under his left arm as my own.

"No, you didn't!" I grabbed it from him and studied it. I remembered every curve and indentation down to the slightest crack in the fiberglass. "Where did you get this?"

"I kept it. You know, to remember you by."

"That's awesome, son." I gave him a hug. "So I take it we can go surfing?"

"Nothing's off limits. Here, put this on." He handed me what looked like a fullsuit, but it was thin and light like a Lycra rash guard.

"You know I don't like rash guards. I'll just trunk it."

"That's a wetsuit. You're not going to believe how warm it is. You're going to need it, too. I checked the buoys, and there must have been some upwelling because the water is really cold for summer."

I grabbed a towel, threw it around my waist, and stripped off my clothes. The wetsuit slipped on like a pair of skintight silk pajamas. Colt was right—it was impossibly warm and flexible. We shared a bar of wax, then ran down the street to the beach access. After a quick paddle out to the break, we were taking turns on the rolling, pristine waves the ocean churned out like a machine. Surfing with my son in perfect waves at an empty break where I'd battled crowds most my life was an impossible treat. It was just like that wonderful, fateful day we shared in Mexico, but the flavor was so much sweeter after everything we'd endured to get there.

Colt caught a long wave, and behind it, the ocean went flat as a lake. As I sat on my board alone, waiting for another set to come, I was overcome by my good fortune. Life sure had its ups and downs, but as long as there was life, there was opportunity, and I was going to make the most of what I'd been given.